TRUTH

Canyon O'Grady leveled his Colt at the three men clustered around the fire.

"Who the hell are you, mister?" the man with the torn Stetson growled.

"A pilgrim seeking knowledge," Canyon said. "Who sent you to murder Alex Koosman?"

"Nobody sent us," the torn Stetson said.

"You just came and shot him dead on a whim?"

"He owed us money and tried to run out on us," the man said after a moment.

There was a sigh of sadness in O'Grady's voice. "Patience is a funny thing. It works in different ways. Consider this. I've tremendous patience with a lovely woman—and none at all with murdering liars."

O'Grady let the hammer of his pistol click. . . .

⊘ **SIGNET** (0451)

JON SHARPE'S WILD WEST

☐ **THE TRAILSMAN #90: MESABI HUNTDOWN by Jon Sharpe.** Skye Fargo finds himself with a woman whose past includes a fortune in silver buried in a lost mine somewhere in the trackless Mesabi range . . . but she can't remember where. The Trailsman must jog her memory while dealing death to the killers who want him underground—not in a mineshaft—but a grave. (160118—$2.95)

☐ **THE TRAILSMAN #91: CAVE OF DEATH by Jon Sharpe.** An old friend's death has Skye Fargo tracking an ancient Spanish treasure map looking for a golden fortune that's worth its weight in blood. What the map doesn't include is an Indian tribe lusting for scalps and a bunch of white raiders kill-crazy with greed. . . . (160711—$2.95)

☐ **CANYON O'GRADY #1: DEAD MEN'S TRAILS by Jon Sharpe.** Meet Canyon O'Grady, a government special agent whose only badge, as he rides the roughest trails in the West, is the colt in his holster. O'Grady quickly learns that dead men tell no tales, and live killers show no mercy as he hunts down the slayer of the great American hero Merriwether Lewis. (160681—$2.95)

☐ **CANYON O'GRADY #2: SILVER SLAUGHTER by Jon Sharpe.** With a flashing grin and a blazing gun, Canyon O'Grady rides the trail of treachery, greed, and gore in search of nameless thieves who are stealing a vital stream of silver bullion from the U.S. government. (160703—$2.95)

Buy them at your local bookstore or use this convenient coupon for ordering.

NEW AMERICAN LIBRARY
P.O. Box 999, Bergenfield, New Jersey 07621

Please send me the books I have checked above. I am enclosing $_____ (please add $1.00 to this order to cover postage and handling). Send check or money order—no cash or C.O.D.'s. Prices and numbers are subject to change without notice.

Name_____

Address_____

City _____ State _____ Zip Code _____
Allow 4-6 weeks for delivery.
This offer, prices and numbers are subject to change without notice.

CANYON O'GRADY

1

DEAD MEN'S TRAILS

by
Jon Sharpe

Ⓢ

A SIGNET BOOK

NEW AMERICAN LIBRARY

PUBLISHED BY
PENGUIN BOOKS CANADA LIMITED

NAL BOOKS ARE AVAILABLE AT QUANTITY DISCOUNTS WHEN USED TO
PROMOTE PRODUCTS OR SERVICES. FOR INFORMATION PLEASE WRITE
TO PREMIUM MARKETING DIVISION, NEW AMERICAN LIBRARY, 1633
BROADWAY, NEW YORK, NEW YORK 10019.

PUBLISHER'S NOTE

This book is a work of fiction. Names, characters, places, and inci-
dents are either the product of the author's imagination or are used
fictitiously, and any resemblance to actual persons, living or dead,
events, or locales is entirely coincidental.

Copyright © 1989 by Jon Sharpe

All rights reserved

The first chapter of this book previously appeared in
Mesabi Huntdown, the nineteenth volume in the Trailsmen series.

First Printing, July, 1989

2 3 4 5 6 7 8 9

 SIGNET TRADEMARK REG. U.S. PAT. OFF. AND FOREIGN COUNTRIES
REGISTERED TRADEMARK — MARCA REGISTRADA
HECHO EN WINNIPEG, CANADA

SIGNET, SIGNET CLASSIC, MENTOR, ONYX, PLUME,
MERIDIAN and NAL BOOKS are published in Canada by Penguin
Books Canada Limited, 2801 John Street, Markham, Ontario,
L3R 1B4
PRINTED IN CANADA
COVER PRINTED IN U.S.A.

Canyon O'Grady

His was a heritage of blackguards and poets, fighters and lovers, men who could draw a pistol and bed a lass with the same ease.

Freedom was a cry seared into Canyon O'Grady, justice a banner of the heart.

With the great wave of those who fled to America, the new land of hope and heartbreak, solace and savagery, he came to ride the untamed wildness of the Old West.

With a smile or a six-gun, Canyon O'Grady became a name feared by some and welcomed by others but remembered by all . . .

The Kentucky-Tennessee border, 1859,
south of Boone's Trace and the Cumberland Gap,
a cradleland of savage history
where today was never far
from yesterday . . .

1

The girl had asked to ride along with him. Amy Powell had a fresh, scrubbed, open-faced prettiness to her; she was part of the wagon train and he'd no reason to say no to her. Until now.

"Canyon O'Grady, that's an unusual name," the girl said, and her appraising stare took in the big man, well over six feet, with a shock of flame-red hair, crackling blue eyes in a roguish face, and a lilt to his speech.

"It is that, and I'm an unusual fellow." Canyon O'Grady smiled but his eyes narrowed as they swept the line of white ash beyond her in the light that was almost dusk. "You get down to the wagons, now, lass," he muttered.

"Why?" Amy Powell frowned in protest.

His eyes stayed on the line of trees. "There's a time for doing and a time for asking. This is a time for doing," he said sharply. "Get your little ass back to the wagons and tell Alex Koosman to make camp in that glen up ahead. I'll be along later."

She hesitated but saw the sternness in his usually roguish face. She quickly sent her horse down toward the five wagons rolling along the old antelope trail below.

Canyon O'Grady returned his crackling blue eyes to the deep stand of white ash. They were still there, the silent, wraithlike horsemen moving through the trees.

They had seen him, of course, decided he was unimportant to their eventual plans, and continued to parallel the wagons below. Their near-naked bodies and saddleless freedom were masks for their perfect discipline. Probably Shawnee, he guessed. His hand stroked the neck of the magnificent palomino he rode, its coppery sheen glistening in the last of the sunlight. He watched the silent forms move on through the trees.

There were men, women, and children in that wagon train he guided, a good and sufficient reason to do his dammedest to protect it. But in addition, he had his own, special reasons, the same ones that had brought him to hire on as an outrider.

He turned the palomino into the trees but hung back far enough to be unseen. The Indians were watching the wagons below and they'd see the camp made in the glen as dusk began to throw its lavender shawl across the low mountain country. The braves would camp also, he was certain. Night attacks were not favored by most Indians.

As dusk grew darker, O'Grady continued to hang back, though he still followed. The Indian band would rest overnight and use the fresh, morning light to make their attack. As the dusk turned into night, O'Grady finally halted, slipped from the saddle, and threw the palomino's reins over a low branch. He waited, sank to one knee, and when the moon began to filter through the trees, moved forward on foot, testing each step.

The pale half-moon gave precious little light through the thick foliage, and Canyon O'Grady relied on his nose as he crept forward. His nostrils flared as he drew in deep breaths and sought the unmistakable, musky odor of damp coonskin and bear grease. Suddenly, as his nose caught the smells, he halted and sank in a crouch as he moved forward again. He moved in quick bursts from one tree to another, his eyes searching the darkness and he finally came to a halt again. They had bedded down without a campfire and O'Grady used the pale moonlight to count the figures that lay on the ground in a ragged circle.

When he finished, O'Grady moved backward with the silence of a diamondback in a pond. He returned to where he'd left the palomino and walked the horse down the slope to the passage at the bottom, where he swung into the saddle again. He rode the half-mile forward to where he saw the half-circle of the wagons, three Conestogas and two big Bucks County hay wagons outfitted with canvas tops.

He entered the half-circle and dismounted. Supper had just ended but one of the women handed him a plate with a chicken leg and beans. He felt the eyes focused on him as he spoke to Alex Koosman, the wagon master. "You've company," he said between bites. "Damn near twenty of them by my count."

O'Grady saw the alarm take instant hold in Alex Koosman's broad, lined face. He was a large man, well on in years but still strong, and his hair still had a blond tone under the gray. He sported heavy, leather suspenders. "We'll have to prepare to defend ourselves come morning," he said gravely.

"You'll have to do more than that," Canyon said, and saw the question come into Koosman's eyes. "You can't let them attack full-force. You'll never stand up to it."

"What else can we do?" the wagon master asked.

"Hit them first. Cut them down before they attack," Canyon said. "I'll want ten men ready to go an hour before dawn."

"I'll pick them out myself," Koosman said.

"The others stay here to defend the wagons in case you still get an attack," Canyon ordered. "Meanwhile, I'll get some sleep. Have your men do the same.

I want them rested and able to shoot straight." He led the palomino to one side of the camp and sat down against the trunk of a box elder and watched Koosman gather his men together. When Koosman finished, he returned to his Conestoga and Canyon's lips pursed. He wouldn't take Koosman with him. He wanted the man here in the relative safety of the wagons. That was important, Canyon murmured to himself as he leaned his head back against the tree and watched Amy Powell come by. She halted, her gaze appraising him again.

"I still want to learn more about Canyon O'Grady," she said.

"Another time, another place, lass," he told her, and she walked away, her trim little rear a joy to watch.

The camp grew still, finally, and he closed his eyes and slept soundly until, with the unfailing, instinctual clock inside him, he woke and saw the half-moon at the far end of the sky. He stood, checked the big army Colt with the ivory grips, and waited as the ten men emerged from their wagons, Alex Koosman one of them. "You stay here with the wagons," Canyon said. "They'll need you if the Shawnee attack."

Koosman obliged and Canyon motioned for the others to follow him as he swung onto the palomino. They filed in behind him as he started up the dark slope, and he led them halfway to the top before he dismounted, gesturing for the men to leave their horses in the thick brush and follow him on foot. He moved uphill again and finally halted. He let the others gather around him. Most were young men, he saw, their faces more determined than grave.

"They'll hear us if we try to get any closer," he said. "Spread out on both sides of the hill. They'll be coming down between us. When I fire the first shot, pour it into them. If we can cut them in half, we've saved the wagons, even if the rest of them still attack."

The men nodded and spread out on both sides of the hill. Canyon settled down in the trees and stayed motionless. As the first gray light of dawn trickled down through the heavily wooded slope O'Grady noted that the others had done a good job of vanishing into the trees. He drew the big Colt as the gray grew lighter and the woods took shape. His hand closed around the ivory grips as he spotted the horsemen slowly moving down the slope. They moved unhurriedly, riding in clusters of two and three except for the one in the lead, a moon-faced brave with a short torso and thin legs. Canyon's eyes went to the markings on the brow band the Indian wore. He had guessed right: Shawnee.

He let the Indian pass and move on some dozen feet while those following came to the center of the slope. He half-rose, took aim, fired, and the first Shawnee flew from his pony in a tangle of flailing arms and legs. The hillside erupted in gunfire. Canyon dropped low as a half-dozen stray bullets smashed into the trees around him. He peered through the leaves and saw the Shawnee wheeling in confusion as they were cut down by the withering cross fire. He paused to take aim again and fire, and another of the Indians toppled backward over the rump of his pony. But the Shawnee that had escaped the cross fire had sent their ponies racing downhill, determined to strike at the wagon train and salvage some measure of victory, something to bring back to the council fires to avoid complete defeat.

"Get to your horses," Canyon shouted at the men, who had mostly broken off firing. He began to run headlong down the slope. A quick glance back showed at least eight slain Shawnee littering the hillside, and when he spotted the palomino, he vaulted into the saddle without a break in stride, the shock of red hair tossing like living flame. He sent the horse streaking downhill toward the gunfire from below, which was interspersed with high-pitched whooping cries.

The wagons and their attackers came into sight in moments, the Shawnee making back-and-forth sweeps in front of the wagons, firing both bows and arrows and rifles. Cut down to less than half their strength, they poured arrows and bullets into the wagons more out of frustrated fury than a serious attempt to storm the half-circle of defenders.

Canyon streaked into open land, aimed, and one of the Shawnee cried out as he fell from his horse. The other men were racing into the open behind him now and the remaining Shawnee wheeled their ponies and broke off the attack on the wagons, unwilling to be caught again in a cross fire. They streaked off in all directions as they fled into the trees.

Canyon pulled the palomino to a halt. Pursuit would be pointless, he realized, and he turned to the wagons with a frown. The Shawnee had poured a lot of fury into the half-circle of wagons. Stray bullets and stray arrows could kill as thoroughly as well-aimed ones, and he felt the stab of relief course through him when Alex Koosman came out from behind his Conestoga.

"Anybody hurt?" Canyon questioned.

"Tom Skew took a bullet in the side, Abe Husack got himself a scraped temple, and Hilda Powell caught an arrow in the leg," Koosman said.

"Hilda Powell, Amy's mother?" Canyon frowned.

"That's right. We can reach Pickett in three hours if we leave now. They can hold out till then, but any longer might be risky. Infection's sure to set in," the man said.

"You can roll," Canyon told him. "There won't be any more trouble from that bunch. They've gone off to get their dead and lick their wounds."

Alex Koosman nodded and hurried off to get the wagons started.

Canyon saw three small knots of figures around the second Conestoga, where Amy looked on nervously. He strolled over and the girl's eyes went to him. "We'll get her to Pickett. There'll be a doc there," he said reassuringly.

"I hear that if it hadn't been for you we might all be dead," Amy said.

"That's about true," Canyon said.

Amusement touched the girl's eyes. "I see you don't believe in modesty."

"Modesty's a vice not a virtue," Canyon said. "It's for those who need it."

"I still want to know more about Canyon O'Grady."

"Maybe, when we get to Pickett. Go see to your ma now," Canyon said. He strode to where Alex Koosman had begun to lead the lead wagon out of the glen. Canyon stood by and watched the five wagons move out. He returned the waves of those on the wagons and wished he'd tried harder to remember their names when he'd been introduced. But it hadn't mattered then and it didn't really matter now. Only Alex Koosman mattered.

Canyon swung onto the palomino and watched Koosman drive his Conestoga, concentration evident in his square, steady, salt-of-the-earth countenance. Maybe the years could give that to a man, he speculated.

O'Grady spurred the palomino forward to ride on ahead of the wagons. His eyes swept the full countryside, ripe with forests and rich land. In the distance, the towering peaks of the Appalachians rose in purple-gray majesty. This was a land steeped in the history of the American nation, a spawning place for legends

15

such as Daniel Boone and the other fighting pioneers who had opened the land westward.

But it was not a land left behind by history's march. In this fertile region, yesterday was today, a place where all the tensions of men's ambitions and men's differences pulsated with living fervor. From south of the Kentucky-Tennessee border came talk and rumors of a separate nation, a confederacy of states, and from north came talk of a new leader and a crusade to abolish slavery. But these were all still distant clouds that could blow away, he recognized, yet the passions and fears of men, the poor and the powerful, were stirred. It all added to the ferment in the land, to the everyday dangers of highwaymen and bandits, hostile Indians and horse thieves, four-legged as well as two-legged predators.

But danger was in his blood—Canyon O'Grady half-smiled—pursuit and death handmaidens of his birth, truth and justice a flame that burned inside him. And this was his land now, this wild and mostly lawless America, and he had brought his own gifts to offer those who cared about right and wrong, truth and honor. It was a grim smile that stayed on his lips as he moved forward, his crackling blue eyes searching the terrain until he found a place where the old antelope trail neared a proper road. He halted, waited for the wagons to come into sight, waved them forward, and waited again until they reached the road. "Stay on it," he called back. He put the palomino into a gallop and soon saw that the road wound and curved its way into Pickett. He rode into the bustling town, asked for and found the doctor, and had the man waiting when the wagons arrived.

While the wounded were helped into the doctor's house, Canyon rode through Pickett and found it to be pretty much the same as most towns, a little neater than the sprawling towns of the Plains country but with enough rowdy and ragged characters of its own. He saw Studebaker seed wagons, plenty of Owensboro mountain wagons with their oversized brakes, and an assortment of buckboards and surreys. Pioneers and mountain men passed through Pickett, but he saw enough small, neat houses to show that the town held a substantial number of good citizens. Further proof was the fact that beside the saloon and dance hall in the center of town, he saw a proper church amid the usual general store and barbershop.

When he finished sizing up the town, he returned to the doctor's house and was told the wagons had camped beyond the west end of town. He found them there, drawn up on a loose half-circle, and Alex Koosman hurried forward as the big redheaded man rode up.

"The doc wants to keep everyone for a few days to see how they're healing before we go on," Alex said.

"That's wise," Canyon replied.

"I've a niece here in Pickett, Adeline Koosman, a lot younger than I am," the wagon master said. "I wrote her I'd stop by when we passed through. Now I'll have a little more time to spend with her. But first I want to buy you a drink, Canyon O'Grady."

"My father taught me never to refuse a good drink or a warm woman," Canyon said. "I've abided by that ever since."

"Good. Jack Wideman and Frank Strawser asked to come along. The whole wagon train's beholden to you, Canyon," the man said. "I'll be right back."

Canyon nodded, and the wagon master soon reappeared on his horse, the two men riding alongside him. Canyon swung in beside the trio and saw Amy Powell watching him from her Conestoga. She offered a small nod as he passed, and he made a mental note to pay more attention to the girl when he returned. She was

17

more than a little curious about him and he liked a curious woman. Curiosity was a powerful force that often carried over into the bedroom.

Alex Koosman's voice broke into his pleasant anticipations as the man reined up in front of the saloon. "It'll be my pleasure, gents," Koosman said, and led the way into the saloon.

Canyon took in the big room, already beginning to fill with customers, though it was hardly past midday. A bar filled one wall with some dozen customers there, and Alex motioned everyone to one of the round tables.

A young woman came to take their order, her face once pretty but now merely empty. "Whiskey," Canyon ordered, and hoped it wouldn't be too undrinkable. Wideman and Strawser ordered the same and Alex Koosman a beer.

"After we left the doctor, I took a minute to stop in and see my niece," Koosman said. "Haven't seen Adeline in ten years. It's going to be nice to have a long visit with her tomorrow."

"None of us might be here if it weren't for Canyon," Jack Wideman said as the girl returned with their drinks.

"Indeed, it was a lucky day when you showed up to sign on as outrider for us, Canyon O'Grady," Alex Koosman agreed, and he raised his stein of beer in a toast.

Canyon took a sip of the whiskey and was grateful to find it strong and rich. He had just taken another sip when he saw the four men as they came into the saloon. The hairs on the back of his neck suddenly grew stiff. Those men spelled trouble. He knew it at once, partly from instinct, partly from experience, and partly from observation. All four had hard, nervous faces and darting eyes, their hands resting on the butts

18

of their six-guns. One with a stetson torn in the brim walked a half-step ahead of the others as they started toward the bar. But Canyon saw their eyes sweep the room in quick but all-seeing glances.

Trouble, Canyon thought again, yet he wasn't prepared for it to erupt the way it did. The four men were almost at the bar when they whirled, almost as one, drawing their six-guns as they did. They poured bullets directly into Alex Koosman.

Canyon cursed as he flung himself backward with the chair, hit the floor, and rolled half under a nearby table, the big Colt already in his hand. But the four men were already racing out of the saloon. Canyon's shot caught one as he reached the swinging doors. The man flew forward with a cascade of blood and spinal bone trailing from the small of his back.

The others were through the doors and outside as O'Grady leapt to his feet and, long legs driving, half-ran and half-leapt across the saloon floor. He burst through the double doors and came to a halt outside. The remaining three killers had disappeared, and he knew they'd cut through between the buildings that bordered the main street. But Canyon moved forward to scan the ground as he holstered his gun. One of their horses had a piece missing in the shoe of his right hindfoot, which left a distinctive print.

Canyon absorbed the fact and went back into the saloon. He knew there was no need to hurry to help Alex Koosman, not with the concentration of bullets they had poured into him, and Canyon cursed bitterly under his breath. He'd made sure to save Koosman from being riddled by Shawnee arrows only to see the man gunned down under his nose.

Damn, Canyon swore silently. His eyes went to Wideman and Strawser as the two men bent over Koosman.

Strawser had tied a kerchief around his upper arm where it leaked a red stain.

Wideman turned to the big flame-haired man, shock still in his eyes. "Jesus, they just gunned him down. He never had a chance. It was plain murder," Wideman said.

"It's called assassination," Canyon said, and drew frowns from both men.

"Why would anybody want to assassinate Alex Koosman?" Strawser said. "Hell, I've known him for six years. He's always been a wagon master, a good, upright man."

"Seems somebody did." Canyon shrugged.

"It had to be a mistake," Wideman put in. "Those bastards just dry-gulched the wrong man."

Canyon shrugged. "Maybe," he said, just managing to keep the grimness from his face. It had been no mistake, he knew. He turned as two men burst into the saloon, the first wearing a sheriff's star on his vest.

"Sheriff Boggs, here," the man said. "You see what happened?"

"Sure did," Wideman said, and Canyon listened as the man recounted the attack. When he finished, the sheriff's lips pursed as he stared down at the bullet-ridden form of Alex Koosman.

"Seems they did what they came to do," he said, and looked at Wideman and Strawser.

"A mistake, it was some kind of mistake," Wideman said again.

"You'd best get to the doc's and have that arm looked after," the sheriff told Strawser, and the man nodded. "You folks decide what you want to do about burying this man. I'll have our undertaker come get him."

"He has a niece in town," Canyon said. "Adeline Koosman. I'm paying a visit to her anyway. I'll ask what she wants done."

The sheriff's brows lifted. "Adeline's his niece?"

"Yes. You know where I'll find her?" Canyon asked.

"Small house a half-mile north of town. She takes in kids for teaching," the sheriff said.

"She's a schoolteacher?" Canyon queried.

"Well, we don't have a proper school so you can't really call her that, but a lot of folks send their kids to her for reading and writing."

"I'll go see her," Canyon said. He turned to Strawser and Wideman. "Looks as though you'll have to pick yourselves a new wagon master."

"I was thinking about you, Canyon," Wideman said at once.

Canyon's smile held just the right touch of rue. "Not me, lads. I'll be getting off here."

"What?" Wideman snapped. "Hell, we'll be needing you even more now."

"Sorry, I signed on with Alex on a week-to-week basis," Canyon said. "He knew I might be pulling out anytime." It was a small lie, unimportant in light of what had happened, Canyon told himself.

"Can he do this?" Wideman asked, turning to the sheriff. "He's a top outrider. He's been dammed valuable to us. We need him."

"A man makes his own agreements. There's nothing I can do to change that," Boggs said.

"You'll find somebody else," Canyon said as he started from the saloon.

"This isn't right. It's not fair, O'Grady," Wideman called after him.

Rue still held in the smile he sent back. "Neither is life, lads," he said, and strode from the saloon into the daylight outside. He climbed onto the palomino, which shook its white-blond mane and went off in an easy trot. Canyon turned the horse north out of Pickett as he still cursed the unexpected turn of things. But maybe it wasn't a completely dead end, he pondered. Maybe Adeline Koosman would furnish something for him.

He slowed as the house came into sight, standing alone under a giant horse chestnut. He scanned the ground outside and saw the small lean-to affixed to the back of the house, a buckboard and a gray gelding under the sloping roof.

He reined to a halt in front of the small house and swung to the ground. No one came to the door and he knocked. He knocked again without an answer. "Adeline Koosman," he called out. "Came to see you about Alex." But silence was the only answer, and Canyon closed one big hand around the doorknob and turned. The door came open and he pushed it a few inches further.

"Adeline Koosman?" he called again, and was rewarded only with silence. He pushed the door open, one hand on the ivory grips of the Colt as he stepped into the house, and found himself in a neat, wallpapered living room. He started to call out again when he heard the muffled sound from another room. He took long, quick strides down a short hallway. The door of the room was open and he halted to stare in at a bedroom and the small figure, bound and gagged, lying across the bed in a torn housedress.

"Damn," Canyon swore. He crossed to the bed in one giant stride, untied the cloth gag across the young woman's mouth, and she let out a deep, sobbing cry of relief.

"Oh, my God," she breathed as he cut her wrist and ankle bonds loose. She sat up at once, the torn top of the dress allowing a glimpse of small, pointy breasts before she pulled herself together. They had done more than tie and gag her, he saw as he took in the red welts on her cheek and forehead.

"Four men," he bit out, and the young woman stared with surprise flooding into brown eyes.

"Yes. How'd you know?" she said.

"They just killed your Uncle Alex," Canyon said.

Horror flooded the young woman's eyes. "Oh, God," she gasped. "Oh, my God." She rose, then sank back down on the edge of the bed. "I was afraid of something like that. I could see they wanted to get to Alex. And I couldn't do a thing. I couldn't even loosen the gag." She paused and focused on the big red-haired man with the handsomely roguish face standing in front of her. "Who are you?"

"Canyon O'Grady," he said. "I was an outrider with your uncle's wagon train." He took a moment to survey the woman with a long glance. She had a short but compact body with small, pointy breasts that almost seemed to have been attached separately. She had a small face, more pleasant than pretty, yet he picked up a certain energetic sensuality to her that was echoed in very full lips. He glanced at her bruises with a frown. "They do anything else to you?" he asked.

Adeline Koosman gave a short, derisive snort. "No, but only because they didn't want to take the time."

"Tell me what they said," Canyon asked.

The young woman rose and paced the room as she talked, her short, compact frame moving with energetic yet not ungraceful motions. "They pushed in and grabbed me when I answered the door. They wanted to know about Alex, whether I'd seen him, whether he was due for a visit, if his wagon train had arrived," Adeline said. "I didn't tell them he'd stopped by, but they wouldn't believe me. That's when they started hitting me."

"And you told them," Canyon finished.

23

"They put a gun to my temple," she said. "Oh, God, I'm so ashamed I told them."

"Don't be. Most folks talk rather than be killed," Canyon said not ungently, and she gave a half-smile of gratefulness. "But they knew he was due in Pickett."

"I never told them. I never saw them before," Adeline said.

"Chances are that Alex talked about coming here. The route was pretty ordinary to Pickett. He talked and they found out."

"Who are they? Why'd they want to kill Alex?" Adeline asked.

"Can't answer that," Canyon said, the reply a half-truth. "But it's plain they left you to go look for Alex."

"Not right away. They searched my place. That's when they found the money, my life's savings, a thousand dollars. I had it in a picture book under the mattress," Adeline Koosman said.

"I saw a bank in town." Canyon frowned.

"It's only been open two months and I hadn't gotten around to going to it yet. They took all of it, damn their thieving hides."

Canyon nodded. They were rattlesnakes, opportunists, hired to do something else but happy to get in a little plain old thievery along the way. He focused his crackling blue eyes on the young woman. "I've some questions for you, Adeline, but they can wait. I'm going after those weasels. If I catch them, I'll bring your money back."

Adeline leapt to her feet and started to fling her arms around the big, handsome flame-haired man but stopped herself and took a step back. "That'd be wonderful, really wonderful," she said.

"You can save it till I get back." Canyon grinned.

"Save what?" she said.

24

"That big hug you were going to give me." He laughed.

Her smile came slowly, a wry appreciation in it. "All right," she said quietly. "You must have been a very good friend of Alex."

"I wouldn't put it exactly that way," Canyon said with a quick laugh. He left her house as she watched him with a quizzical stare.

2

Canyon sent the palomino back to town and to the saloon, where he halted to peer at the print still plain on the ground, the broken section of shoe an indelible mark. He followed the prints and saw the horse and rider had turned into an alleyway between buildings, the others racing on ahead of him.

Canyon cast a glance skyward and saw there was still enough daylight left as he followed the hoofmarks. The trio had continued north and gone into hill country thick with red mulberry and bur oak. Confident that they'd done their job well, they made no effort to cover their trail. Canyon allowed a grim smile: overconfidence was the mark of small minds.

The day began to slide into dusk and Canyon saw that the trio had slowed their pace to a walk. He wasn't more than a mile behind them, he estimated, and the copper-hued palomino had hardly drawn a long breath. They'd camp soon, he was certain. He followed the prints with extra care as the last of the light began to fade.

When the night came, he reined up and swung to the ground. But he'd noted that the three killers had been moving along a narrow pathway, probably an old Saux-Fox trail. He followed along the pathway until he spotted the flickering light of a small campfire. He draped the palomino's reins over a low branch and went forward alone, the Colt in his hand, fingers closed firmly around the ivory grips.

Canyon crept forward through the thick underbrush, careful as always to make each step silent as a bobcat on the prowl. But the care was almost unneeded. The three figures lounged around the small fire, passing a pint bottle of whiskey from one to the other. The thought of pursuit was nowhere in their collective thoughts.

I know, Canyon murmured silently to himself. Common sense says I ought to take these three down with one volley, leaving one wounded so he can talk. But even a polecat deserves a chance to save itself, he argued silently. Besides, I've never been one for gunning down a man in cold blood. With a sigh, he broke off the silent conversation. He leveled the Colt, ready to fire, as he lifted his voice, his tones quietly firm.

"Surprise, gents," he said. "Nobody moves, nobody gets killed." He saw the three figures stiffen but stay in place. "That's good, very smart indeed. It's satisfying to see such a display of good sense," Canyon added almost pleasantly.

"Who the hell are you, mister?" the man with the torn stetson growled.

"A pilgrim seeking knowledge," Canyon said from within the bushes.

"What the hell does that mean?" the man snapped in irritation.

"It means I want to know who sent you to murder Alex Koosman," Canyon said.

The three men exchanged quick glances.

"Nobody sent us," the torn stetson said.

"You just came and shot him dead on a whim?"

There was a moment of silence. "He owed us money and he tried to run out on us," the man said.

"That's not even inventive. Try the truth this time," Canyon said.

"That was the truth," the torn stetson insisted.

There was a sigh of sadness in Canyon O'Grady's voice as he replied. "Patience is a funny thing. It works in different ways. Consider this: I've tremendous patience with a lovely woman and none at all with murdering liars." He let the hammer of the pistol click, the sound loud in the darkness. "You've one more chance."

The three figures stayed silent for another instant, and obviously at a hand signal flashed between them, they erupted, diving away from the fire in all directions.

Canyon's first shot caught the nearest one as he rolled toward the bushes, and the man gave a jiggling little motion and came to a stop. The second one was in the middle of a flying, headfirst dive into the brush when Canyon's second shot caught him in midair. The man's body buckled, his legs drawing up. He half-turned in the air before dropping to the ground on his face. But the one with the torn stetson had made it into the brush, where he lay still.

Canyon crept behind the trunk of a bur oak, the Colt in his hand. "All I want is some answers," he called out. "Get smart."

The reply was a hail of bullets that slammed into the tree trunk. Six shots, Canyon counted, and he knew the man had to reload. He took the moment to break from behind the oak, run, and dive headlong back into the brush, a dozen feet closer to the figure in the bushes. He crouched, his eyes on the row of bushes across from him, as he refilled the Colt. The man wasn't the kind to take on a one-to-one shoot-out, especially against someone who was plainly a crack marksman. He was crawling away in the bushes, but it was impossible to see the leaves move in the darkness. Canyon moved his eyes to where the three horses were standing, and he rose to a crouch, then darted quickly in a half-circle to bring himself around to the far side of the horses, where he dropped to one knee.

He had only to wait for another few moments when the man appeared at the edge of the bushes. Still on hands and knees, he crawled around the front of the horses and started for the far side, unaware that O'Grady was waiting there.

When he rose beside his horse, Canyon leveled the Colt, took aim at the man's shoulder. He still wanted answers. "Hold it right there," Canyon called.

The man whirled, firing as he did, the reaction not unexpected. Canyon let the Colt bark. His aim perfect, he saw the man clutch at his shoulder and fall backward. The curse froze in his throat as the man hit the ground right under his horse. The animal bolted and the horse's hooves came down hard. Canyon heard the sickening sound of skull bones being crushed and stomped into tiny bits. He stared down at the prostrate figure on the ground that resembled a doll with the head smashed in.

"Dammit to hell," Canyon swore, turning away for a moment. The man would not answer anything ever.

Canyon returned to the two figures closer to the fire. He emptied their pockets, found nothing, and finally had to return to the third one, who lay in a slowly spreading pool of red. He found Adeline Koosman's money in the man's shirt, pulled it out, and stuffed it in his trouser pocket.

With an angry sigh, Canyon turned and made his way back to where he'd left the palomino, swung onto the horse, and rode back down the narrow pathway. He retraced his steps, not hurrying, and he let his thoughts unreel, his mind become a wheel turning back to what had brought him to this lush, dense Kentucky-Tennessee land that was stained with blood, old and new.

He was back in the richly furnished room with the cherrywood desk, the inlaid writing table to one side and the United States flag in one corner. He was back in Washington again. He'd been inside the White House before, with its four great columns along the front, but his assignments usually came from one of the army staff officers.

But not this time. This time he'd been called into the dignified inner office where the man in front of him wore a black frock coat, afternoon trousers, and a stiff white collar with a matching winged tie known as a "stock." The man, over six feet in height, gazed at his visitor with sharp blue eyes. His pure white hair came to a tuft just above his forehead and he carried his head cocked slightly to one side. But it didn't diminish his air of authority. This man was the distinguished James Buchanan, President of the United States.

"I wanted to see you personally on this, Canyon O'Grady. And I've been wanting to meet you for some while," President Buchanan had said. "Besides, we've something in common."

"We do, sir?"

"Yes. My father came here from Ireland, just as yours did," the President had said. "But I didn't call you here because of sentiment," he added, growing more firm. "We only have a half-dozen men who carry the title of U.S. government agent, and word has it that you're one of the very best."

"I try." Canyon had smiled.

"I'm told you can charm, think, or fight your way out of most anything, O'Grady."

"The luck of the Irish, Mr. President." Canyon had grinned.

James Buchanan had smiled back. "With the sixth sense of a cougar and the skill of a backwoodsman . . . But let's get to the matter at hand. Does the name Meriwether Lewis mean anything to you, O'Grady?"

"Of Lewis and Clark?" Canyon had asked, and the President had nodded. "They're already famous in every history book," Canyon went on. "They pioneered trails across the Rockies, mapped out the Columbia and Missouri rivers and a lot of smaller ones, and blazed a trail to the Pacific. They were the greatest of explorers and pioneers in all the West."

"That's right," Buchanan had said. "But a lot of people don't know that Meriwether Lewis was appointed governor of the Louisiana Territory after the Louisiana Purchase. Furthermore, there was serious talk of his becoming the first governor when the territory became a state."

"No, that's not as well known," Canyon agreed. He had seen a touch of sadness come into James Buchanan's face.

"It's also not known that Meriwether Lewis was a man subject to strange moods. He had great fits of melancholy, sometimes actual derangements. He was often very depressed by the world around him and the nature of his fellow men. Yet he was a brilliant man and very much admired by many, including Thomas Jefferson." President Buchanan had paused, taken a glass of water from a carafe on the desk, drank half, and gone on. "In October of 1809 he decided to make a trip to Washington from Louisiana. He never reached here. On October 11 he was killed in an inn in Tennessee. He was found alone, a pistol in one hand, and no killers were ever caught."

"I do remember reading something about that," Canyon had said.

"Some well-known people, including President Jefferson, felt that Meriwether Lewis hadn't been murdered but had killed himself in one of his fits of depression. They all remembered his increasingly black moods. Others felt he'd been murdered by backwoods thieves—there were a number of hoofprints found outside the inn—but to this day, no one knows whether Meriwether Lewis killed himself or was murdered on his way to Washington."

Canyon had regarded the President and turned the man's words in his mind. "You seem to feel there might be reason he'd be killed on his way to Washington," he had suggested, and drew a faint smile from James Buchanan.

"Yes, there are things that make us think that, and now still more things have been happening to make us suspect that," the President had said. "But I've only set the stage. It's much more complex than what I've said so far. That's why I asked you here, O'Grady, to give you a chance to find out the truth about what happened to one of America's greatest pioneers and explorers."

Canyon recalled having nodded with excitement. But there had been a lot more, and when President Buchanan had finally finished, Canyon had realized the dimensions of the puzzle and he had but one comment. "You might never get the final answer, Mr. President," he said.

"I know, but then you may get enough other answers to put that last one together," the President had said. "Good luck to you, Agent Canyon O'Grady."

Canyon's thoughts snapped off and returned to the dense countryside and the dark night. Once again he realized that he was pursuing pieces of yesterday that had come alive today. Only now one piece had been snatched away in front of him. He had hoped to learn things from Alex Koosman. The man had been one of the last of his leads, and now Koosman could join the others on the list of names he carried in his saddlebag. "Look on the bright side, lad," Canyon muttered aloud to himself. "Good luck has a way of following bad." He smiled at the self-administered advice. It wasn't a completely closed door. The threads still entwined among one another. He had only to find the right one.

The dark outlines of the buildings of the town came into sight. He turned the palomino north and found the small house under the horse chestnut with only an hour or so of night remaining. He reined to a halt outside the house, dismounted, and the front door opened before he reached it.

Adeline Koosman's small face peered at him with concern. "I couldn't sleep. I was worried about you."

"I'm grateful." Canyon smiled and walked into the house, where a thin candle gave a flickering light. He reached into his pocket and tossed the roll of bills on the small coffee table in the living room.

Adeline's eyes grew wide and her voice caught at a sharp gasp. "You got it," she squealed.

"All of it. They won't be bothering you again."

This time she didn't hold back as she flung her arms around him and clung tightly against him. He felt the small points press against him through her nightdress. "I'll never be able to thank you enough," she murmured as she clung to him until she finally pulled back, her eyes searching his face. "You must be exhausted," she said. "I've an extra room with a good bed in it. Sleep here and we'll talk tomorrow."

"That sounds mighty appealing," Canyon said.

"This way," she said, and spun on her heel. He

33

followed her down the short hallway, eyeing a small but compact rear that moved nicely under the night-dress. She halted at a small room with a single bed in it and a dresser. "Sleep as long as you like," Adeline said.

"I'll take that advice." Canyon nodded and she hurried away as he began to pull off clothes. He stretched out naked on the bed and let his powerfully muscled body relax. The bed was narrow, just barely able to accommodate his big frame, but he offered a long, contented sigh at its softness. "A lullaby for the senses," he murmured, his eyes closed. He fell asleep with dawn just peering over the hilltops outside.

He slept soundly and the sun was at the noon hour when he woke, saw the big porcelain basin filled with water atop the dresser, and washed and dressed. When he went outside, he found the house empty, but a piece of paper lay on the kitchen table, weighted down with a pewter tankard. He read the message scrawled on the paper in a thick, crayon-like pencil: "Gone to town to get supper vittels. Be back soon. Adeline."

He went outside and unsaddled the palomino to let the horse roam in the sun, its magnificent coat shining as though it were copper. He spotted a small well near the back of the house, took a dandy brush and curry-comb from his saddlebag, and began to give the horse a good cleaning. He worked slowly, unhurriedly, doffing his shirt. He had almost finished when Adeline rolled up in the buckboard. He saw her eyes move across the powerful symmetry of his body and he helped carry the bags of groceries into the house with her. She wore a light-yellow blouse that rested provocatively on her pointy breasts, and he noticed again how her short, compact body moved with its own energetic grace.

"I'd say a good meal is the very least I can do for you, Canyon O'Grady," Adeline said.

"I won't be saying no to that."

"I brought back a good leg of pork. I'll start things to cooking right away."

"And I'll finish with the horse." Canyon returned outside. When he finally ended his grooming, the delicious aroma of pork over the fire and turnips and collard greens cooking wafted out to him. He tethered the palomino on a long rope that let the horse almost circle the house, and he went inside as the day began to wane. He sat down in a cane chair and watched Adeline as she puttered in the small kitchen.

"It's seldom I get the chance or the urge to do real cooking," she said.

"You look as though you're enjoying every minute of it."

"I am," the young woman said, following with a bright smile. "I suppose there's no chance of your staying around, is there?"

"None. Too much unfinished business waiting," Canyon said.

"I thought that might be too much to hope for," Adeline said. There was ruefulness in her half-smile, but a kind of determined cheerfulness along with it. She was plainly someone who took life as it came without letting the world get her down, and she had an appealing winningness to her. "Maybe you'll come back this way," she said brightly.

"I just might."

"Meanwhile, I've some good Tennessee sippin' whiskey."

"I'm for that," Canyon said. The whiskey, when she poured it from a clay jar, was indeed rich and tasty. "Tell me about your Uncle Alex," Canyon said as he sat back and savored the whiskey.

"There's not much to tell. I hadn't seen him for some ten years, though he'd write a few times a year. He was a nice man, a good relative. He was my favorite when I was a little girl," Adeline said, memories flooding into her face.

"Can you think of anything else about him?"

"Why are you so curious about Uncle Alex?" Adeline asked, a furrow coming to her brow.

"Just wondering why anyone'd want him dead," Canyon answered.

Adeline frowned into space for a moment. "There was one thing: he worked for the government once, a long time ago. I remember him saying that one time."

"The men who came here looking for him, they say how they knew he'd be visiting you?" Canyon asked.

"No, but I'm sure Alex told a number of people he'd be visiting Pickett. That was his way. He was a very open person."

"Not about everything," Canyon commented. "He had some secrets, and he was killed for them."

Her brown eyes became grave. "I guess so," she said. "But none I knew about."

Canyon nodded. He believed Adeline Koosman, an open ingenuousness about her.

She speared him with a sidelong glance as she frowned in thought. "You know, Canyon O'Grady, I've a feeling you know more about my Uncle Alex than I do," she said.

He put his head back as he laughed. "Not really, Adeline," he answered, sending a wide, warm smile her way. He'd not tell her anything more. She had almost become a casualty already. There was nothing to be gained by plunging her more deeply into it. "I could stand another drink of that fine sippin' whiskey," he said.

"All right," Adeline said. "I'd rather have memories, anyway.'' She had another with him and still another over dinner, which turned out to be more than ordinarily tasty.

''You're a fine lass with a kettle, Adeline. I'm surprised no man has made off with you yet,'' Canyon told her as he helped clean away the dinner plates.

''Enough have tried. Maybe I'm just too particular,'' she answered with an edge of defensiveness in her voice. ''Guess I take after my grandmother. She never found the right man at the right time.''

''You will,'' Canyon said gently.

''You'll be moving on tomorrow?'' Adeline asked, and he nodded. ''But you'll stay the night here, won't you?''

''I'd like that,'' Canyon said. His hand came up and curled around the back of Adeline's neck, a warm, sensuous touch. She moved to him, lifted her arms, and her full lips found his mouth in a warm, lingering kiss. He swung her up into his arms, his lips still holding hers, and he stepped into the bedroom where he had first seen her. He placed her down on the wide bed and she pulled her lips back from his, a tiny smile touching her face, an almost impish quality to it.

''Surprised?'' she asked teasingly.

''No.'' Canyon laughed and she offered a pout.

''That's unfair. Why not?''

''Every flower blossoms in its own way, and if you've seen enough blossoms, you learn the signs.''

''And you've seen a lot of flowers blossom,'' she snapped tartly.

''Enough,'' he said softly.

She studied him with a sidelong appraisal. ''I wish there was time to learn more about you, Canyon O'Grady.''

''You can make a start now,'' he said, and let his fingers open the top button of the yellow shirt. She made no move to stop him and he went down to the others, undoing each one until the shirt hung loose. Adeline wriggled her shoulders and the shirt came away.

The smallish, pointy breasts stood out firmly, almost aggressively, each tipped by a pink nipple that also pushed out firmly against a small, light-pink circle. Adeline pushed on her skirt and it slid from her, along with some white bloomers. She drew her legs up, half-turned, and lay back on the bed.

Canyon's eyes moved over her compact body, the slightly convex little belly, short waist, and strong hips. Her legs were graced by the firmness and vitality of youth and a deep tuft of moss lay over her pubic mound. Altogether, Adeline Koosman exuded an energetic sensuality, a vibrancy that was its own kind of beauty, a small triumph of the spirit over the flesh.

Canyon pulled off clothes as he felt excitement growing inside him. Adeline's hands were upon him at once, moving like eager, exploring little butterflies up and down the hard, muscled contours of his body.

"Oh! Oh, my God," Adeline gasped as her hand came to his burgeoning, pulsating warmth, and she drew away instantly only to return with another gasp.

Canyon lowered his face and drew one of her pointy breasts into his mouth. Adeline gave a shuddery little cry of delight. He sucked the small, soft mound, felt the firm pink tip under his tongue, and her fingers closed harder around him as she gasped. He let his lips continue to caress the breast while his hand moved slowly down across the convex belly and onto the deep tuft.

Adeline gave tiny cries of delight, small pieces of sound someplace between a gasp and a cry. When his hand moved still farther downward, pressing into the soft-firm flesh of her inner thighs, the tiny sounds suddenly became a long groan. Her legs fell open and her compact torso pulled in and then thrust upward, her body calling out with its own language.

He drew his mouth from her breast as his fingers curled into the dark, secret places, and as he touched her lubricious lips, Adeline summoned a half-scream of sheer pleasure. Her hips lifted again, but he stayed at the very tip of the portal, touching the fervid spots of sensitivity. Adeline's half-scream became a full cry. Her breasts jiggled and their small, conelike mounds thrust upward at the same time. "Go on, go on," Adeline cried up. "More, more . . . take me."

Canyon touched deeper inside the moist passage of pleasure. Now Adeline's cry was almost a sob and her hands dug into his back as her compact form rose up, her torso thrusting, her hips gyrating first to one side, then the other.

He swung himself over her, let his own straining eagerness come to her and slide smoothly and deeply, filling, touching every part of her warm, wet tunnel. "Oh, oh, my God . . . aaaaiiiii," Adeline cried out, and her hips began to pump and thrust. In a moment all of her torso joined in as she gasped out with his every matching motion. Her strong, compact thighs lifted and locked around him. She rolled with him as she lifted and twisted, thrust and pulled, and all the while the small, shuddery sounds came from her. "Ah, ah . . . oh . . . oh . . . aiiieee . . ."

Adeline gasped and rolled and heaved and thrust with him, using her compact body with a kind of energetic abandon until, when his own moment was upon him, she arched upward with a sweeping surge of ecstasy. "Now, oh God, now, noooowwww . . ." Adeline screamed as he pulsed within her. She clung tight against him as her scream became first a groan of fulfillment and finally a sob of despair. "Oh, oh damn

. . . damn,'' Adeline murmured into his chest. "Why couldn't it last longer?"

Canyon smiled down at her and found himself thinking of an old expression from a faraway land and a faraway time. "A hungry sparrow is a fierce sparrow," he said gently, and saw the tiny smile edge her full lips.

She brought his hand to curl around one of the smallish breasts, uttered a sigh of contentment, and closed her eyes. She slept wrapped in his arms and he let himself find sleep beside her. But when the dawn came, he woke as he felt her hand moving down his powerful body, halting at his maleness. They came alive again until finally her screams of ecstasy filled the small room and, with the morning sun, she slept hard again in his arms.

He woke with her when the sun streamed full into the room and he heard the rapping on the front door.

"I'll answer it," she said, and slipped on the yellow shirt, which hung down to her midthighs.

He reached out as she swung from the bed, found a towel, pulled it around his waist, and strapped his gun belt over it to keep it in place. He was in the doorway, one hand on the butt of the Colt, when Adeline opened the front door and he felt his brows lift in surprise. A young woman stood just outside the door. She was immensely attractive even at a quick glance, and Canyon saw her eyes go to Adeline and then to him.

"I came looking for a Canyon O'Grady," she said.

"You found him," Canyon answered, and saw her eyes, a very light blue, take on a veil of disapproval.

"I see," she sniffed. "I'm sorry. I didn't expect I'd be interrupting anything of this sort."

"You didn't." Canyon smiled brightly. "My compliments on your timing."

The disapproval stayed in the light-blue eyes. "An

accident, I assure you. And perhaps a mistake," she said, and turned on her heel.

Adeline closed the door as the young woman stalked away. She was already halfway back to the bedroom when the knock came again, three sharp, demanding raps. Adeline returned to the door, pulled it open, and the young woman's eyes went past her to Canyon.

"I do have to talk to you. I've no choice," she said, her lovely face set. "I'm at the inn, Crawley's Bed and Board." She spun around again and stalked off.

Adeline held the door open until the young woman swung onto a brown mare with a white blaze and rode away.

"What was all that about?" Adeline frowned at Canyon as she closed the door.

"Dammed if I know," he said, took off the gun belt and towel, and began to dress.

"But you're going to find out, of course," Adeline said, and Canyon smiled at what he heard in her voice.

"I wouldn't be a gentleman if I didn't."

"If she were fat and ugly, would you be so concerned about being a gentleman?" she tossed back waspishly.

Canyon's smile broadened. What was it about a night of pleasure that brought instant possessiveness, he wondered silently, more amused than annoyed.

"Of course," he answered Adeline. "And if I didn't, may the shame of all gallantry be upon me."

Adeline returned a cynical glance even as a tiny smile found its way into her voice. "You're so full of charm, Canyon O'Grady, you almost have me believing you," she said. When he finished dressing, her arms encircled his neck. "Come back if you change your mind about going on."

"Indeed I will," he said, giving her a long kiss before he hurried outside to the palomino.

3

Canyon O'Grady rode slowly into town, found Crawley's Bed and Board, and dismounted. In her disapproving haste, the young woman had neglected to leave a name, and he halted before a stoop-shouldered man beside an old desk. "I was asked to meet a young woman here. She gave me her name on a slip of paper, but I went and lost it. She's fairly tall, attractive, with a lot of thick black hair," he said.

"That'd be Room Two. She said someone might come asking for her. Just down the hall," the clerk said.

Canyon stepped down the corridor and quickly found the faded room number stenciled on the door. When he knocked, the door was opened almost instantly and he saw the young woman regard him with a mixture of relief and cool appraisal in her light-blue eyes.

"Were you afraid I wouldn't come?" Canyon asked with a smile.

"You're very perceptive," she said, her eyes narrowing. "Let's say I wasn't sure. You did seem preoccupied."

"Perhaps I was just changing clothes. You could be jumping to conclusions," Canyon said.

Her smile was condescending. "I hardly think so," she said, and opened the door to the room wider. He stepped in as his eyes stayed on her. She had taken off

42

her outer jacket and wore a white tailored blouse underneath that pushed out atop a pair of well-rounded, full breasts with a fine curve to their undersides. "You've a bold eye, Canyon O'Grady," she said.

"Bold?" He frowned. "Not at all. Since when is the appreciation of beauty bold?"

"And a touch of blarney to go with the boldness, I see," she said.

"No blarney at all, only truth. I see hair beautifully black as a raven's wing, eyes the color of a morning lake, skin the milk white of snowberries, and a body a goddess would be happy to call her own," he said, words of charm but also of truth. She also had a straight nose, finely etched lips, and thin, black eyebrows that had a perpetual half-arch. It all managed to give her face a combination of softness and hauteur.

She allowed a small smile at his description and gestured to a chair. "Please sit down. I'm sure you want to know why I came to see you."

"First I want to know how," Canyon said. "How did you know where to find me?"

"Sheriff Boggs told me," the young woman said, and Canyon's eyes stayed on her. "You told him you were going to pay a visit to Alex Koosman's niece."

"So I did."

"You see, I really came to Pickett to see Alex Koosman," she said. "When I heard he'd been shot down, I asked the sheriff about it. He told me you'd been there and that he'd heard you were an outrider for the wagon train and knew the countryside. He said you'd saved the wagons from a Shawnee massacre but you'd quit the train. That's when I decided to come look for you."

"All right, that's how. Now, why?"

"I need your help to find my father. I have to warn him," the girl said, suddenly very grave.

"Warn him?" he repeated with a frown.

"It had to do with Alex Koosman," she said. "I came to see if he had any idea where my father might be."

"They were friends?" Canyon asked, and felt the stab of excitement inside himself.

"Yes," she said, and the stab of excitement became a spiral.

"What's your name, lass?" Canyon asked.

"Jennifer . . . Jennifer Shell," the young woman answered, and Canyon had to act quickly to keep his face impassive. "You see, Sam Shell, my father, and Alex Koosman were old friends, lifetime friends. Two years or more ago, my father up and left and hid himself away someplace up in this country, maybe in the Appalachians, maybe in the Cumberlands. I thought Alex Koosman might know."

"So when you heard he was taking a wagon train through Pickett, you hurried here to meet him," Canyon said.

"Yes." She nodded, her lovely face darkening with pain. "Only I was too late."

"One door never closes but another opens," Canyon murmured.

"Meaning what exactly?" Jennifer Shell snapped. The comment had been made more for himself than her. The name of Sam Shell was one of those on the list in his saddlebag. But she was quick to pick up on the unsaid, he saw.

"You lost Alex Koosman, but you found me," Canyon explained smoothly, and she turned the reply in her mind for a moment.

"Yes, I suppose that's true enough," she said, finally. "It does seem to work out that way sometimes."

"This seems to be one of them."

"I know I'll never find him on my own. I don't know the land and I don't know what I might run into. I'll pay you well to help me."

"Why do you have to warn your pa?" Canyon asked, sliding the question out almost casually.

"He was one of seven men who were all close friends many years ago. Five of them have been killed during the last year and now Alex Koosman makes the sixth one. That leaves only my father, and I don't know if he knows about any of this. He's been off by himself for years, moving around, doing odd jobs."

"How'd you come to learn of it?" Canyon asked.

"I stayed on at the house after Pa left and I kept getting these death notices in the mail. I didn't pay much attention to them at first, and then I began to realize that these were all men he used to talk about, all his old friends. I began to get worried. When the fifth death notice reached me, I knew something was wrong. I mean, it was too much of a pattern."

"That's when you decided to try to find your pa," Canyon offered.

Jennifer nodded vigorously. "Will you help me? I told you I'll pay you well."

"Never turn down a lady in distress."

"Thank you," the young woman said, and he heard the sincerity in her voice.

"One question bothers me: what makes you think your pa didn't leave because he was afraid of something?" he asked, keeping the sharpness from his voice.

Jennifer Shell frowned into space for a moment. "I don't know, not for sure. But I don't think so. He left over a year ago, before any of the killings started."

"Just a thought," Canyon said, and put her answer aside. Sam Shell could have had intimations, or word might have filtered to him. Or Jennifer might be right:

perhaps he had just left and knew nothing. Or perhaps Jennifer was being coy and careful. He snapped off thoughts as her question came to him.

"When can you leave?"

"Right now."

"Give me fifteen minutes," Jennifer said.

"I'll be waiting outside," Canyon said, and walked from the inn. But when he climbed onto the palomino, he felt the tiny prod of misgivings behind the smile. It had all seemed too easy, too fortuitous, and he always distrusted things that came too easily, whether it was money or women. But then, he wasn't about to look a gift horse in the mouth, either. If lovely Jennifer knew more than she'd told him, he'd find out along the way.

He was relaxed in the saddle when she appeared from the rear of the inn on a brown mare with a white blaze, a sturdy-enough horse, he noted. Jennifer had changed to a checked blue-and-white shirt and a leather riding skirt that allowed a view of long, beautifully curved calves.

"You have anything to help us?" Canyon asked.

"In his last letter to me he said he was in the Cumberland Mountain forest. He had a cabin there and he wrote me he'd made some friends, hill people," Jennifer said.

"We'll find him. I know a cut through high hill country that'll get us to the Cumberland with days saved," he said, and sent the palomino northeast in a steady trot.

Jennifer Shell rode well enough, he saw, but with formal school training that placed an emphasis on posture, a straight back, arms at exactly the right position. He let her ride that way for an hour before he turned a tolerant smile on her.

"You'd best relax some or you'll be falling out of that saddle by tomorrow," he said, not ungently.

She made no reply but she did let go of the stiffness.

The terrain was thick with shagbark hickory and black walnut with heavy underbrush yet enough broomsedge to afford grazing forage for the horses.

When Canyon paused at a small brook to let the horses drink, he slid to the ground and refilled his canteen. Jennifer followed his example and he watched the grace of her long body as she bent to the brook.

"There's one thing I forgot to mention," Canyon said almost offhandedly. "From now on, when I say left, you go left. I say jump, you jump. I say quiet, you be quiet. In short, I give the orders. These mountains and forests are no place for debates and discussions. Things happen too fast."

"Is that the only reason?" Jennifer asked, the thin black eyebrows lifting higher than their usual arch.

"There can be only one captain on a ship," Canyon said.

"Then that ought to be me, seeing as how this is my venture and I hired you."

"You hired me for what I know and what I can do. You hire a man to bring in a stallion, you let him do it."

Her lips pursed as she thought for a moment. "We'll talk more about this."

"I won't," Canyon said, and his smile did nothing to dilute the firmness in his voice.

"Is that an ultimatum?" Jennifer Shell bristled, the light-blue eyes gathering ice.

Canyon's affable smile stayed. "An ugly word, that. Never liked it. Call it advice, the kind you'd best take if you want me along."

She returned a wry smile. "You do have a way with

47

words, Canyon O'Grady,'' the young woman said as she swung onto the brown mare.

He returned to the palomino, aware she'd not given any word of agreement. He let the palomino set its own pace, and Jennifer rode beside him. He noted the number of thoughtful and curious glances she threw his way as they rode.

Before the light faded, he drew one of the new Henry rifles from its saddle case and, with one shot, brought down a plump cottontail.

''Supper,'' he said as he hung the prize from rear jockey saddle strings. He sent the palomino up a low hill and began to sing in a strong, clear tenor, a jaunty, spirited tune.

> ''As I was sitting by the fire,
>   talkin' to O'Reilly's daughter,
> Suddenly a thought came into my head,
>   I'd like to marry O'Reilly's daughter . . .
> Kiddee-i-ay, kiddee-i-ay, kiddee-i-ay
>   for the one-eyed Reilly,
> Kiddee-i-ay, kiddee-i-ay,
>   try it on your own big drum.''

Jennifer broke in after he'd sung the third verse. ''You're in good spirits,'' she remarked. ''Considering what may lie ahead.''

''The best of healers is good cheer, so said an ancient Greek poet named Pindar,'' Canyon answered, and he pointed to a pair of black walnut that leaned toward each other to form a small bower. ''We set down for the night up there,'' he said.

Jennifer followed him up the incline as the day began to trickle away and he tethered the palomino inside the bower and began to skin the rabbit.

''I'll gather firewood,'' Jennifer offered, and he

gestured to where a patch of slender, quill-like leaves grew. "Pull up some of those wild onions, too," he said.

Using a razor-sharp hunting knife, he worked quickly and deftly, and by the time night came, the rabbit was on a makeshift spit over a small fire, the slivers of wild onion embedded into the tender meat.

Jennifer sat back on her elbows and he watched the way her beautifully curved breasts pushed upward against the checkered shirt. Her thin black eyebrows arched slightly as she regarded him with faintly amused eyes.

"I want to know what makes Canyon O'Grady tick," she said.

"Why, pray tell?" Canyon laughed.

"Because you're more than you make out to be," Jennifer Shell said, and Canyon let his smile mask his thoughts. She was sharp, probing, yet right now she was more curious than suspicious, he decided. "You're plainly no ordinary outrider or scout. You're a man of some reading who can quote ancient Greek poets. You're quick, astute, obviously very good at whatever you do, and you use your charm and your Colt with equal ability, I'm sure."

"You can't judge a book by its cover," Canyon deferred.

"Exactly. That's why I want to see past the cover. Start with your name. Canyon O'Grady . . . How'd you come by it?"

"My mother gave it to me." He smiled cheerfully.

Her eyes narrowed with a moment of irritation as he turned the rabbit. "All right. How and why?" she pressed.

"She was always reading books and looking at paintings about America. I was close to being born when my father told her we were fleeing Ireland to go to America. She wanted to give me a name that fit the breadth and spirit of America, and so she came up with Canyon. Of course, Father Rearden would have none of that. So he baptised me Michael Patrick O'Grady, but my parents never called me anything but Canyon.''

"Your father was fleeing to America? From the great potato famine?''

"Yes, but mostly from the British constabulary. He was one of the founders of the Young Ireland Movement and a close friend of Fintan Lalor and Padraic Pearse. That alone was enough to have the British after him. When he fled, they had a price on his head, but then the English have been putting prices on Irish heads since Cromwell. So he came here with a new-born baby with a name that was a nod to yesterday and tomorrow.''

"Canyon O'Grady," Jennifer murmured, rolling the name on her tongue. "It's a wonderful name indeed.''

"My father joined the work gangs that built the rail-roads throughout the East, but as I grew up, I knew that would never be for me. I wanted something with more adventure in it. So I went west, into the new frontier.''

"Did your father ever go back to Ireland?''

"Twice. Took me with him both times, partly as a cover," Canyon said. "He stayed for two years each time.''

"Being part of the revolutionary movement," Jennifer put in.

"Now, I didn't say that." Canyon grinned. "But he put me into the hands of a group of wise and learned friars who poured everything they knew into this visitor from America. You can blame the good friars for any education that still shows.''

"I'll do that," Jennifer said. "But none of this tells

me much about the man who rides the most beautiful palomino I've ever seen.''

Canyon's glance went to the magnificent copper-toned horse. ''He is a beauty.''

''What do you call him?''

''Cormac.''

''That has a meaning, I take it?''

''Indeed it does. King Cormac was one of the four great Irish kings of the eighth century,'' Canyon told her as he leaned forward and took the rabbit from the spit. ''Supper's ready for the eating,'' he announced, and Jennifer hungrily joined him in the meal, made tastier by the wild-onion seasoning.

When they finished, Jennifer sat back on her elbows again and Canyon enjoyed the way her full-cupped breasts turned upward. She sent a half-chiding smile his way. ''I was thinking as we ate,'' she began. ''I've never had anyone tell me so much that was actually so little. It was all charming history and I still know nothing about Canyon O'Grady here and now.''

Canyon laughed. ''Are you so hard to satisfy in everything, Jennifer Shell?''

''About most things,'' she returned, the thin black brows in a cool arch, and he laughed as he rose and put enough dirt on the fire to put it out. A half-moon took a few moments to cast its pale light onto the heavy forest land, and when it did, Jennifer pushed to her feet, went to the brown mare, and took her night things from a canvas. She disappeared into the black-ness of the trees and he heard her undress as he took out his own blanket and set it on the ground.

He had his shirt off when she returned in a light-blue loose cotton nightgown that tried to hide the full curves of her figure and failed. He saw her eyes move across his chest, take in the hard-muscled symmetry of his torso with an appreciation she couldn't hide. "You're welcome to share my blanket," he offered.

"You're too kind," she said with no attempt to disguise the sarcasm in her reply. "I've my own, thank you." He shrugged and began to walk from the bower. "Where are you going?" she asked quickly.

"Just for a little walk. I often take little walks before I turn in," Canyon said. "You stay here and go to sleep. You need anything during the night, you wake me."

Jennifer's frown held a touch of cool amusement. "Am I to take this as one of your orders?"

"You could," Canyon said blandly.

"My sleeping habits hardly seem a subject for one of your orders."

"They are now," Canyon returned, and he felt her frown follow him as he walked from the bower. He pushed his way through black walnut and thick brush to find a rise just beyond the bower. He halted and drew in a deep breath. It was still there, stronger, more defined than he had detected a little while back. Sharp, yet with a hint of muskiness, the odor of a male mountain lion on the prowl.

Canyon carefully pushed his way up to the top of the low ridge and saw it led down to a section of wide, flat rocks. He halted and let his eyes slowly scan the length of the ridge; he saw no sleek, stealthy form, but he knew that meant little. His nostrils told him the big cat was somewhere in the vicinity, and he finally turned and retraced his steps to the bower.

Jennifer, her eyes closed, lay on her side on her blanket, and he saw her breasts move up and down in the steady breathing of sleep. He lay down on his own blanket, shed the rest of his clothes down to his underdrawers, and put the big ivory-gripped Colt down alongside him. He felt tiredness sweep over him, the flesh demanding relief, and he closed his eyes and was asleep in moments.

He had no idea of how long he had slept when he suddenly wakened, his eyes blinking open. That inner watch that never slept—what some called an inner consciousness and others a sixth sense—had snapped him awake. Something was wrong. He felt it inside himself and he had long ago learned never to ignore the signals from within. He rose onto one elbow, craned his neck to look across at Jennifer, and swore as he saw only the empty blanket.

He leapt to his feet, pushed the Colt into its holster, pulled the big Henry from its saddle case, and ran from the bower. He moved through the brush and up the small rise, instinct telling him it would beckon her that way. The half-moon cast a pale silver glow across the top of the ridge, and he pushed upward on long, powerful legs. He was almost at the top when he suddenly heard the sounds, half-whimpered, breathy gasps, and then he heard the other sound, the low, vibrating growl, the embodiment of pure predatory fury, a sound that had not changed since the age of the saber-toothed tiger.

Both sounds came from the other side of the low ridge. Canyon crested the rise and dropped to one knee to stare down at the scene just below him. Jennifer, her back against a tall rock, her face wreathed in terror, faced the long, sleek tawny form not more than six feet away from her. Her lips were parted, Canyon saw, the tiny, gasped whimpers falling from her open lips, and he raised the rifle and lowered it again. The angle was bad, the mountain lion directly in front of her. A miss in the poor light could hit the girl.

Canyon's eyes went to the big cat and saw the tip of its tail twitching, always a certain danger sign. Yet there was still a chance . . . if she did nothing to trigger it into action.

"Stay still. Don't move . . . don't run." Canyon hissed the words under his breath, hoping that somehow, someway, he could send the message on invisible waves of thought. But the hope failed. The terror that had frozen Jennifer in place also made her erupt in panic. He couldn't blame her. She didn't realize that if she stayed absolutely still, the mountain lion might well turn away. It hadn't been hunting her. She had just gotten into its way.

But Jennifer was staring directly into the cougar's eyes, he knew, looking into the twin amber pools of death, an experience that had unnerved many a mountain trapper who should have known what to do. The scream tore from Jennifer's throat at the same instant she started to fling herself sideways from the rock. The big cat reacted instantly to become a tawny streak of fang and claw. It landed on Jennifer as she reached a flat rock. She fell face-forward screaming.

Canyon fired, not taking the time to aim. It was the effect of the shot he wanted, anyway, and the big cat whirled at once at the explosion of sound, instantly found the figure on the ridge, and with a single, seemingly effortless bound, disappeared into the rocks and high brush beyond the ridge. Canyon raced down the other side of the ridge to where Jennifer lay on the rock and reached her in seconds. "Oh, my God, oh, God," he heard her gasping out as he halted beside her quivering body.

"Stay still," he said, his eyes on the back of her nightgown, which was ripped open, and the red that seeped into the shredded garment. He peered at the long marks that ran down the upper part of her back, and uttered a grunt of relief. "It's not too bad. It didn't really tear in before the shot caught its attention," he said. "But it'll have to be treated."

Canyon reached down, started to lift her when she came into his arms, still quivering, tiny sobs welling up from her graceful throat. "It's over," he said soothingly, and held her against him and felt the warm, soft curves of her breasts. "Can you walk?" he asked, and she nodded and drew back, her light-blue eyes searching his face.

"I'd be dead, torn apart, if you hadn't been there," Jennifer said.

"Most likely." Canyon rose to his feet and pulled her up with him.

She swayed a moment, straightened, but was very willing to let his arm stay around her waist as he started up the side of the ridge. He held her to him, reached the top of the ridge, and started down the other side. The side of one breast pressed into his arm, beautifully soft and full. There was a redeeming feature to be found in most everything, Canyon noted silently.

When they reached the bower, Jennifer slid to the ground in a combination of emotional and physical shock.

"Stay on your stomach," Canyon ordered, the soothingness gone from his voice. "And take down the top of that nightgown. I have to get at your back." He strode to the palomino, rummaged in the saddle-bag, and returned to Jennifer carrying a small, cork-stoppered clay jar.

Jennifer had pushed the top of the nightgown to her waist but had bunched it in front so it covered her ribs and breasts completely.

"Modesty, no matter what, eh?" Canyon commented.

She said nothing and he knelt beside her, surveying her nicely rounded shoulders, her long back and her supple skin firm and taut where it dipped into the narrowness of her waist. He unstoppered the jar and began to rub the ointment over the claw marks on her back.

"Aaaaah . . . that feels good," Jennifer breathed.

"White vinegar wash with arrowroot, balm and fuchsia," he said, smoothing the concoction carefully into each open wound and then massaging with gentle pressure over the rest of her back as he searched for knots and swollen muscles. But there were none. The cougar had had its claws no more than halfway out when it pounced. "You're lucky," he grunted, and Jennifer answered only with little sighs of pleasure as his hands moved up and down her back. But when he reached the small of her back and the edge of the nightgown he felt her stiffen at once. "That'll do it for now," he said. He pushed to his feet and returned the jar to his saddlebag.

Jennifer had half-turned, the nightgown clutched in front of her when he came back from the palomino. Her eyes followed him as he dropped down on his blanket. "Thank you, Canyon O'Grady," she said. "I know that's quite inadequate for what you did."

"Get some sleep," he said gruffly, and she lay back on her blanket and fell silent. The aftermath of shock quickly wrapped itself around her and she was asleep and breathing heavily in moments.

He turned on his side and pulled sleep around himself. The other things he had to say could wait till morning.

4

"You're angry with me, aren't you?" Jennifer said when she returned from the brush in the leather skirt and a yellow shirt that caught the morning sun.

Canyon, tightening the cinch under Cormac didn't glance at her as he answered. "Now, whatever gave you that idea?"

"I told you my back hardly hurts this morning, I thanked you again for last night, I asked if you wanted me to do anything, and you haven't said one word to me," she said, and managed to sound hurt.

Canyon straightened up and speared her with an icy stare. "Not one word? Well, now, I'll try to correct that at once," he said grimly. He had wrestled with how he'd handle her. He needed her every bit as much as she needed him. But he couldn't let her suspect that. "Now, why would I be angry with a gorgeous colleen such as yourself?" he slid at her. "Because you almost got us both killed last night? Because you went off to show me you weren't about to take orders you didn't want to take?"

"I couldn't sleep. I decided a little walk would help me get back to sleep," Jennifer protested with a glower.

"Doing it was bad enough. Lying about it is worse. You went off on purpose. I think they call it asserting your independence. I call it asserting your stupidity."

Her lovely lips tightened. "Maybe that was part of it."

"That was all of it," he barked, refusing to let her hide in a half-truth.

She lifted her light-blue eyes to him. "All right, I should've listened to you. I'm sorry, I really am."

Canyon kept the wry smile inside himself. She had her own strength. An apology and an admission of guilt but no promises for the future. He decided not to push her any further for the moment. She'd learned a lesson that would stay with her. He regarded her thoughtfully for a long moment. "I've never been one not to allow a person one mistake," he said with more loftiness than he'd intended.

She flared instantly. "Don't be condescending to me, Canyon O'Grady," she snapped back.

"You've a temper to add to it," he said, meeting her angry glare.

"I don't like being treated as a child."

"Then don't act like one," he tossed back, and drew an angry glare. He kept the stiffness in his face but he was content to let her have her standoff. "Maybe we ought to start over."

"Yes, please," she said at once, relief in her voice. "I'll do better, I promise."

He let his face soften. "A bargain sealed is a bargain made," Canyon said.

"Yes," Jennifer agreed, and quickly offered a handshake.

He took her hand and pulled, and she half-fell into his arms as his mouth pressed down on the finely etched lips. Soft, pliant, responding automatically, she returned his kiss for a moment as the very tips of her breasts touched his chest, and then, stiffening, she pulled back. "Now, that's a much better way to seal a bargain." Canyon smiled broadly. "More personal, don't you think?"

"I think it's an excuse for taking liberties," Jennifer said sternly.

"I never do that."

"Take liberties?"

"Make excuses." He laughed and swung onto the palomino. He watched her mount the blaze-faced mare, moving with supple grace, her breasts pulling the yellow shirt tight for an instant to outline their loveliness. She came up alongside him as he took the palomino into the low hills, a terrain heavy with box elder, black walnut, and sugar hickory with thick high brush, plenty of violet wood sorrel and dove weed. He found a stand of wild plums and walked the horses as they breakfasted. "Tell me about Jennifer Shell when she's not out chasing down her father," he said.

"Back home in Arkansas she takes in boarders," Jennifer said. "Pa wanted me to keep the house when he took off. It's a decent living, he told me, with plenty of traveling folks looking for a clean place to stay. He was right."

"Didn't you think anything about his just taking off like that?" Canyon asked casually.

"Not really. He'd done it before, gone off by himself. It was something he just did sometimes," she said.

Canyon let himself appear to accept the answer. It was possible Sam Shell was just indulging his own wanderlust. But it was equally possible he'd heard enough to send him fleeing. That would matter a lot, but only after he found Sam Shell. He turned off thoughts and concentrated on moving through the thick wooded hill country. He fell silent as he rode, and his gaze swept every gulley, peered hard into every furrow of land, probed along each stream, and scanned each break in the low brush.

Aware that Jennifer frowned as she watched, he suddenly reined up sharply, a glint of satisfaction in his eyes. "There it is," he said, and pointed to a spot at the edge of a clear stream.

"There what is?" Jennifer asked.

"A trap line," Canyon said, and Jennifer finally saw a part of the jagged jaws that lay half-buried by the stream. "We follow it and we find the trapper."

"We're looking for my father, not trappers," Jennifer said with a touch of testiness.

"We'll never find him by wandering about and hoping we get lucky," Canyon answered. "Who knows what goes on in these hills better than anyone else?"

"Trappers," Jennifer muttered.

"Exactly, the men who roam and work these hills every day of every year." Canyon moved toward the partly hidden trap beside the stream. He slowly turned and followed the stream, spotted the next trap and then the next, and at each one he saw Jennifer look away, her face tight. "Never did take to trapping, myself," he said. "A hunter's good, clean kill is something different. But keeping an animal trapped in pain for days, that's not for me."

"Maybe they'll find a better way someday," Jennifer said. She closed her eyes when they passed a trap with a beaver in it, the animal's right hind leg all but crushed by the steel jaws of the device.

Canyon hurried on and finally reached the top of the trap line and dismounted to examine the footprints that led to and away from the lead trap.

"I'd say there'll be a trapper's cabin about a mile due north," he said. "Lead your horse."

He moved forward, Jennifer beside him, and he guessed they had gone perhaps a half-mile when he smiled in satisfaction. A thin line of light-gray smoke rose straight into the air about a quarter-mile on.

He let Jennifer see the smoke and slowly moved forward again.

When they drew close enough for him to smell fish cooking, he put a hand on Jennifer's arm. "This is as far as you go," he said. "You stay here with the horses."

He saw her mouth open to protest and speared her with an icy stare.

She pulled her mouth closed and glowered back. "It's not fair. I've a right to see and hear what goes on," she muttered.

"Many trappers don't see a woman for a year or more. They get a look at you and you'll damn well see and hear what goes on," Canyon said. "Follow in my footsteps."

He set off through the woodland, aware that her glower followed also. He moved quickly yet silently, using the patches of star moss that covered a good part of the moist forest terrain. As he neared the cabin, the cooking odor grew stronger and then he heard the voices. He listened, counted two, then a third. He grimaced as he pushed on. He would have preferred a lone trapper happy for company and glad to be talkative. He halted, turned to Jennifer. "You stay here," he said, and she glowered back.

"I can't see or hear from here," she murmured.

"I'll fill you in on everything," Canyon said, and he hurried on. He straightened up and began to stride through the woods, making no effort to be quiet now. He even took to whistling a tune, and when he reached the clearing, he pushed his way through the trees and halted, obvious surprise flooding his face.

The three men watched him as he appeared, behind them a roughly built cabin, an open fire with a kettle on it to one side, and the cabin walls hung with pelts on pegs. Three number-one bear traps were on the ground, one open with an oil rag alongside.

Canyon's eyes returned to the three figures. All wore unkept beards, and one, with a floppy-brimmed, dirty hat with long black hair sticking out from under the brim, held a heavy Smith & Wesson Volcanic rifle. The second, standing in dirty long johns, held an old Kentucky long rifle while the third, wearing only Levi's, held a skinning knife. Two were thin, of medium height, also wearing thick, uncombed and straggly black hair, and all eyed him with a mixture of curiosity, suspicion, and hostility.

They saw he was no trapping man, Canyon knew, and he offered a wide smile. " 'Morning, friends. Canyon O'Grady's the name," he said cheerfully. He drew no return smile.

The tall one with the floppy-brimmed hat answered. "Crabbly, Cy Crabbly. These are my kin, Rufus and Herb." Cy Crabbly's small black eyes peered at him, a piercing stare. "You're either lost or you be taking a helluva long walk, mister," the man said.

Rufus and Herb snickered but there was no humor in the sound of it.

"Maybe some of both, friends," Canyon answered, and his eyes flicked to the cabin again. He saw the door hanging by one hinge, the lone windowpane broken, garbage strewn along the bottom edge of the structure. The Crabblys were a slovenly lot, he noted. "I'm looking for a man, name's Sam Shell," Canyon said.

Cy Crabbly tilted his head to one side in an appraising stare. "You be a sheriff?" he asked.

"No, no." Canyon smiled. "I'm an old friend of his."

"If you're such an old friend, how come he didn't tell you whar he was livin'?" Cy Crabbly queried, and

Canyon kept his smile. They had a crafty sagacity in spite of their rudimentary intelligence.

"He did tell me," Canyon answered. "But I wrote it down and lost it a while ago. I heard he had a place up here somewhere and I expect you boys would know it if he did."

Herb and Rufus set their rifles down and returned to work, Rufus kneeling down beside the spring mechanism of the open trap, Herb turning to brushing the pelts on the wall. They had plainly decided to leave the decisions to Cy.

"If he did, we ain't sayin'," Cy Crabbly answered.

"I don't call that friendly," Canyon remarked mildly.

"I don't care what you call it, mister," the man said, a rasp coming into his voice. "Folks up here go their own way. We keep it like that."

"Sure I can't get you to change your mind?" Canyon asked.

The man's lips edged a sneer. "You get yourself on, mister, afore we lose our good manners."

Canyon eyed the other two. They were far enough from their rifles and Cy Crabbly had his long-barrel Volcanic pointing downward, held casually in the crook of one arm. But he didn't want to explode in a fusillade of gunfire, Canyon reminded himself. He wanted at least one able to answer his questions, and a shoot-out might end that. He was still searching his mind when Rufus leapt to his feet beside the open trap. "Be still," he snapped while he peered into the trees. Rufus frowned, his already low brow made still lower by the deep furrows, as he peered hard into the trees and his nose twitched furiously as though he had become a scraggly, two-legged rabbit.

Suddenly, with a half-cry, half-oath, Rufus charged forward with surprising quickness, hurtled headlong through the trees and brush, and vanished from sight almost at once. His short oath of triumph echoed back, and he appeared a moment later, dragging the figure with him.

Canyon caught a flash of jet-black hair streaming backward and a yellow shirt. He felt the curse explode inside him.

"Lookeee, lookeeé here," Rufus shouted in delight. "Lookeee what I found spyin' on us."

"I'll be dammed," Cy Crabbly muttered, and his eyes devoured Jennifer with a quick glance.

The third brother had come forward to gaze at her with a smile that oozed anticipation.

Canyon saw Cy Crabbly's small black eyes turn to him, the man's face growing hard under the floppy-brimmed hat. "This little kitten with you, mister?" he asked.

"Never saw her before," Canyon said as he swore inwardly. "She looks like a mountain girl to me," he added, unable to think of anything else.

Cy Crabbly spat. "That's beaver shit, mister, and you know it. I think she's with you." The man peered hard at him, and Canyon shrugged away the remark. The man's face broke into a grimace of a smile. "Don't make any real difference," he said. "She's ours now."

Canyon remained outwardly relaxed as his stomach churned and he watched Cy Crabbly raise the rifle to point directly at his stomach.

"Get his gun, Herb," the man ordered, and Herb reached over and lifted the Colt from its holster. Canyon smiled as Herb admired the ivory grips and shoved the gun into the waistband of his torn Levi's.

"You boys are making a mistake," Canyon said calmly. They'd never let him leave alive, he realized. He'd have to make a try, and there'd be but one chance. His eyes swept the scene again, grew cold as they passed Jennifer, who tore her wrist from Rufus' grip. Canyon took in the three men as he maintained his outward calm. Though they were far from mentally swift, they were woodsmen and their physical reactions would be instant. He had to do something to disrupt them, distract their reactions for an instant, something different enough to give him the precious moments he'd need. As he clicked off thoughts, he heard Jennifer find her voice.

"He's telling the truth. I don't know him," she said.

"Shut up, girlie," Cy Crabbly snapped. "I don't believe a damn word out of either of you."

As Canyon looked on, he saw Rufus reach a hand out and squeeze Jennifer's breasts.

"Look at these, Cy. We're going to have us a fine old time." Rufus laughed, and Jennifer knocked his hand away as she shrunk back.

Canyon edged slowly toward where Herb stood near the open trap, but he halted as Cy speared him with a sharp glance.

"Where do you think you're goin', mister?" the man snarled.

"You told me to get myself out of here," Canyon answered, still keeping his voice and manner mild.

"That was before," Cy snapped. "Now you're going noplace. I just got to decide whether we skin you first or let you watch us enjoy your little kitten."

"Filthy pigs," Jennifer bit out, her eyes light-blue flame.

Cy Crabbly turned back to her with a twisted smile. "Spirit. I like that in my pussy. Right, boys?"

"Right. You got it, Cy, you got it," the other two chorused.

The three of them had their eyes on Jennifer, who glared back. It was possibly the only moment Canyon would have, he realized. He had to take it. Herb was closest to him, and that was good. O'Grady grunted silently, his muscles tightening as he gathered himself.

His leg kicked out, a straight, hard blow that slammed into Herb's thigh. The man pitched forward, his leg landing in the trap, and Canyon heard the snap of the steel jaws as Herb Crabbly's scream rent the air.

Cy and Rufus spun around to stare down at their brother as he writhed on the ground, one leg in the trap and his screams of agonizing pain.

Canyon sprang into action at once; his arms closed around Rufus from behind and he swung the man in front of him just as Cy whirled and fired the rifle. Canyon felt the bullet smash into Rufus, felt the man's body shudder and smash back against him.

With a roar of surprise and fury, Cy Crabbly charged forward, but Canyon's hand, already around Rufus' body, yanked the Colt from the man's waistband. He let the human shield, now a limp weight, fall away, and before Cy Crabbly could halt his charge and bring the rifle up to fire again, the Colt barked three times. The three bullets slammed into Cy Crabbly with split-second rapidity, and the floppy brim of his hat shimmered and shook. The trapper did a sudden, loose-limbed dance before collapsing to the ground in a heap that shook once more and lay still.

Canyon glimpsed Jennifer to one side, on one knee, while Herb Crabbly's screams continued to spiral into the air. Canyon was at his side in two long steps and saw the steel teeth of the trap protruding through the man's legs from one side to the other.

"Jesus, get it open," the man gasped out between cries of pain. "Help me, Christ, help me."

"After you answer some questions," Canyon said calmly, and saw Jennifer approach.

"Get the trap open first. Jesus, the pain . . ." Herb cried out.

Canyon shook his head. "You talk first. No talk, no trap."

"My leg, it's killin' me," Herb groaned.

"Sam Shell, did you see him?" Canyon asked.

"Jesus, yes, yes," Herb Crabbly gasped out. "He came to visit sometimes. Oh, Jesus, my leg."

"Where'd he live?" Canyon questioned.

"A cabin," Herb said.

"Where?"

"North . . . toward Black Mountain," the man said. He made a futile pass at the trap with one hand and fell back onto the ground again. "Get it off me, Jesus, please!"

"How far?" Canyon persisted.

"Day's ride, maybe two," Herb groaned.

Canyon knelt down and seized the two jaws of the trap. He pulled them open as the man screamed again.

Herb Crabbly pulled himself from the trap, using his arms to crawl across the ground, and then he fell forward, breathing and groaning sounds coming from him.

"Get the horses," Canyon said to Jennifer.

"Jesus, you can't leave me, not like this," Herb said, pushing up on one elbow. He looked down at his shattered leg, which streamed blood. "Jesus, help me," he implored.

"You three would've killed me and screwed the girl to death. You've horses tied up in the back," Canyon said. "Maybe you can get to one. I'm giving you more chance than you'd have given me, and more than you give the animals you trap in those things."

Jennifer returned with the horses, and Herb Crabbly pounded the ground with his fist between gasps of pain. "You bastard," he cursed at O'Grady.

"Be right back," Canyon said to Jennifer. "I want to have a look inside." He strode into the cabin—

nothing specific in mind, except to see if the trio had anything worth taking. The interior of the cabin resembled a pigsty more than it did a house, and Canyon swept the disarray with a quick glance. He saw nothing of interest amid the clutter and was about to turn away when a small wooden box in one corner caught his eyes. He kicked aside empty cardboard boxes as he went to it. His eyes narrowed in thought as he stared down at the dozen or so sticks of dynamite. He took six sticks, tied them together tightly with an extra length of fuse cord, and strode from the cabin.

Outside, Jennifer frowned at the dynamite as Canyon tucked the sticks into his saddlebag, but she said nothing. He climbed onto Cormac as Herb Crabbly crawled another few inches and halted to writhe in pain.

"No, you can't leave me," Herb insisted again, but Canyon beckoned to Jennifer with a nod and she climbed onto the brown mare and set out after him as he sent the palomino into the trees. He headed north at once, stayed on narrow, winding deer trails, and set a hard pace until he halted some hours later to rest the horses at a stream.

"I only came in closer to hear," Jennifer said. "I don't understand it. I stayed down low. He couldn't have seen me."

"He didn't," Canyon snapped. "He smelled you." Jennifer's frown was protest. "He smelled powder and skin oil, maybe hair rinse. That's why I told you to stay back. A good trapper has a nose damn near as good as the animals he hunts."

Jennifer's lips pressed tight against each other. "I'm sorry."

"Seems I've heard that before," Canyon said. "It's not likely you'll get a chance to say it again."

"I'll remember that, I promise," Jennifer said, and he returned to the saddle.

"Mount up. We've a hard day's ride left," he said, and kept his word by setting a fast pace until night fell. They camped in the deep of the Cumberland Mountains.

Jennifer curled herself inside her blanket and Canyon undressed quickly and slid into his bedroll. He pushed away the thoughts that tried to intrude, and plunged into hard sleep.

5

The new day came and Canyon O'Grady woke with the warm sun. He was washed and dressed when Jennifer woke, in the saddle when she returned after changing. He set a hard pace again, and when he halted at a lake to refresh the horses, Jennifer's eyes searched his chiseled countenance.

"You worried about things?" she asked. "You're hurrying real hard suddenly."

"We've been running into delays. The men that killed Alex Koosman were only hired guns. Somebody's directing this, somebody with maybe more information than we have."

"The kind of information that could send another pack of hired guns to the cabin and Daddy."

"Exactly. And you have no idea why they'd be after your pa," he slid at her.

"I told you I didn't."

"So you did," Canyon said. "It slipped my mind."

"I doubt anything slips your mind." Jennifer's thin, black eyebrows arched. "I think you don't believe me."

"That's a harsh thing to say, lass," Canyon said. He looked hurt as he climbed onto the palomino and sent the horse forward. He glanced back to see Jennifer atop the white-faced mare, starting to hurry after him. She caught up quickly as he rode more slowly now, and at every break in the trees he halted to sweep the terrain below and above with a long, steady stare. At one point, as the day began to drift toward a close and he halted on a protrusion of land that afforded a sweeping view of the terrain, Jennifer's voice held despair in it.

"It's like looking for a needle in a haystack to find a cabin in these mountains," she murmured. "You can't see anything but trees and more trees."

"It takes practice," Canyon said.

"What does?"

"To see instead of just look," he answered. "Those trees aren't solid. There are breaks all over. The natural ones form a certain pattern, the deer and moose trails another, and the ones made by man form another. Men make roads very different than moose or deer do. They make a clearing for a cabin very different from the way nature forms a clearing."

"You see something?" Jennifer asked.

He pointed downward and on another mile or so. "Let's have a look over there," he said, and sent the palomino forward. He moved down the hillside toward a path of hackberry that rose up along another hill to his left, rode through the trees to where a narrow road had been worn, swung the horse onto it, and followed its almost straight path. He slowed at places and gestured to Jennifer as he peered at tree branches. "A deer trail has low branches worn down or snapped off in an irregular pattern. These have been cut away," he pointed out to her, and she nodded as excitement touched her face.

The day had begun to darken when Canyon slowed the horse as, through the trees, he spied the small cabin, the ground in front and on both sides cleared away.

He drew the palomino to a halt and slid to the

ground, his eyes narrowed as he peered at the small house. It was a quiet place, nothing moving, no smoke from the short chimney, no horse tied nearby. Canyon watched, waited, and finally edged closer.

The door to the cabin was closed but not latched, leaning against the frame. A small milk pail lay over-turned near the door. Canyon rose, drew the Colt, and motioned for Jennifer to stay back. In a half-dozen quick strides, the flame-haired figure was at the cabin, yanking it open and dropping low at the same time.

Only emptiness and silence greeted Canyon O'Grady. He rose to his feet and beckoned Jennifer to move forward. He waited at the door for her and went inside when she reached him, his eyes sweeping the single room that was the cabin. A cot rested against the far wall, three shelves on the other wall, only an empty wooden cup on one. Three wall pegs hung empty, Canyon noted, and he stepped farther into the cabin and saw the faint layer of dust over the floor. A torn burlap sack lay in one corner; he paused to ex-amine a pair of boots with the soles beyond repair.

Odd towels and pieces of torn shirt lay scattered in one corner, along with an old cotton blanket. "Some-body lived here not too long ago," Canyon said. "And cleared out, took everything with him." His lips pursed in thought. It could have been Sam Shell. Then it could have been someone else. The cabin was in the right area, yet perhaps there was another.

Jennifer's excited half-scream burst into his thought. "It was him," she called. "He was here." Canyon spun to gaze at her as she held up an empty packet of pipe tobacco. "This is his, the brand he always smoked."

Canyon smiled. "Half a victory, lass," he said. "We found the place, but he's gone."

"Half a victory? Don't you really mean no victory?" Jennifer asked, disappointment in her voice.

"No, I mean what I said. Now you know he was alive not too long ago."

"Yes, that's true," hope coming into Jennifer's voice at once. "And maybe we can pick up a trail from here."

"I'd hope this might jog your memory a little more," Canyon said. "And I'm wondering why he cleared out."

"You think he knew about the others?"

"Can't say." Canyon shrugged. "But a man doesn't just pick up and clear out all of a sudden. I'd say he heard something—talk, questions, word of men looking for him." Jennifer frowned into space. "The same questions stays," Canyon added, and she turned to him.

"What same questions?" she asked.

"Why is he running? What's he afraid of? Why were the others suddenly killed? There's got to be a connection someplace," Canyon said with disarming casualness as he watched Jennifer. But there was only perplexity and dismay in her face. He caught no glimpse of furtiveness, no quick attempt to hide a moment of alarm. Perhaps she didn't know anything more than the conviction that her father was in danger. But even if she didn't, she had to wonder by now. Of course, she'd not admit that, and he'd not press her on it now, he decided. There'd be time enough for that.

The little cabin began to grow dark and Canyon saw a candle on a trencher beside the fireplace. "Bring your things in," he said, and when she returned, the candle was lighted, a flickering glow extending a dim light inside the cabin. "You take the cot. I'll use my bedroll on the floor."

"You are a contradiction, Canyon O'Grady," she

said. "You were heartless back with those trappers and now you display gentlemanly chivalry."

"I'll answer that with the words of your American poet, Walt Whitman. 'Do I contradict myself?' he asked. 'Very well, then, I contradict myself. I am large. I contain multitudes.' "

Jennifer let a slow smile move across her finely etched lips. "And you fascinate, I'll admit. You make me want to find out more about you, Canyon O'Grady."

"Sounds promising." He smiled.

"Not that way," she quickly said.

"When you explore, you never knew where it'll lead you," Canyon returned cheerfully, and he strode outside and took his bedroll from the palomino. He tethered both horses along one side of the cabin and paused to survey the dark bulk of the trees that rose up on all sides, the moon not yet high enough in the sky to shed its pale light. An uneasiness stirred inside him and his skin had grown prickly, part of those inner senses he had long ago learned not to ignore.

He had found the cabin. Others could, also, more easily if they had better information. His eyes grew narrow as he peered into the deep forests. Alex Koosman had been gunned down not all that far away. Perhaps there was more than one band of hired searchers, Canyon pondered. He'd not take chances.

He returned to the palomino to take a spool of fairly strong mending thread from the saddlebag. But he'd no cutlery, no tin cans, nothing to use, he grimaced unhappily. He'd have to fall back on Mother Nature, he decided as he began to take the thread and string it from tree to tree at the edge of the clearing, no more than six inches from the ground. When he stepped back, he couldn't see it himself. He drew another length of the thread and knotted it onto a section of the horizontal line of thread and pulled it up to a low thin, young tree branch. He wrapped the thread tightly around the end of a short piece of lariat and used the lariat to bend the tree branch backward.

Working with slow care, he relaxed his grip on the branch, gingerly tested the pressure, adjusted it again, and finally stepped back as the branch held in place. If the thread were broken, it would spring back with hard-enough force to wake him, he was sure, and he finally returned to the cabin.

Jennifer, on the cot in the loose blue nightgown, eyed him with a narrow glance. "You took an awfully long time out there. What were you doing?"

He had already decided that the less she knew, the better he'd like it for the moment. "Thinking," he answered. "Communing with the night. It helps renew the spirit."

"How poetic," she sniffed skeptically while he set his bedroll on the floor.

"You're sounding shrewish, lass. You're tired. Go to sleep," he said, and blew the candle out. He undressed to his underclothes and stretched out on the bedroll in the blackness of the cabin. She was tired, he knew, and he listened to her fall hard asleep in minutes.

He catnapped, let an hour go by before he rose and silently pulled on clothes. When he'd dressed, he rolled his bedroll and took it with him as he slipped from the cabin. He silently closed the door behind him and circled to the rear of the cabin, where the tree branches almost touched the roof. He picked out a sturdy basswood, used one arm to carry the bedroll and the other to climb. He pulled himself up on a branch, edged to the end, and dropped onto the roof of the cabin, landing on the balls of his feet and silent as a lynx.

There was only a slight pitch to the roof, and he

spread the bedroll out and lay down on it. He let himself sleep, but when he disciplined himself, sleep was never an absolute. Like the horned owl that hooted in the distance, his inner sense was always awake.

The night drew on into the deep hours just before the dawn when suddenly Canyon's eyes snapped open. The sudden half-brushing, half-slapping sound penetrated to that inner sense to bring him awake instantly, and he immediately knew it for what it was, the branch torn loose to spring back into the leaves of the tree.

It meant only one thing: the thread he had drawn around the trees had been broken. He rolled onto his stomach, the Colt in his hand, and peered down over the top of the roof to the ground below. In the dimness of the moon's last light, he saw the figures at the edge of the trees where one had unknowingly snapped the thread. He counted six as they halted at the edge of the cleared land. They waited and finally moved forward again, and Canyon saw one raise a rifle to his shoulder. The man fired, the shot a sharp, loud sound in the stillness of the night as the bullet thudded into the closed door of the cabin.

"Sam Shell," the man called, and lowered the rifle. "Come on out of there."

Jennifer didn't answer, but her gasp came up through the chimney at his shoulder. "Canyon," he heard her say.

"Come on out, Sam," the man called again.

Jennifer's voice, a harsh, whispered sound, came up to Canyon through the chimney again. "Where are you?" she asked. "Dammit, answer me."

Canyon's eyes stayed on the dim shapes below. "No one's gonna hurt you, Sam," the man called out. "Somebody just wants to ask you some questions, that's all, just a few questions."

Canyon's lips tightened. There was more unsaid than

said in the man's words. Sam Shell was the last of the seven. It was obvious they wanted him alive and able to talk. Of course, he'd only stay alive until they got what they wanted from him. But for the moment, Canyon realized, it gave him an advantage. He didn't have to pull punches. Jennifer's voice came up through the chimney to interrupt his thoughts.

"He's not here," he heard her gasp out in a hoarse half-whisper. "Damn you, Canyon O'Grady. You picked a fine time to run out."

The man's voice came again from below and Canyon peered down over the edge of the roof. "We'll just stay till you come out, Sam," the man called. "You're going to have to come out. You know it and we know it. Now, why don't you save us both a lot of trouble?"

The cabin remained silent. Canyon waited while the last of the moonlight disappeared; dawn would follow soon enough, he knew. He listened to the sounds that drifted up the chimney from inside the cabin.

Jennifer was pacing back and forth, muttering, "Damn you, Canyon O'Grady," from time to time as she did. She'd pause for a spell, then erupt again in further pacing and muttering.

But Canyon saw the first light of the new day begin to slide across the sky, and he edged toward the end of the roof, brought the Colt up ready to fire. Jennifer had stayed quiet and let them think it was her father in the cabin, and Canyon hoped she'd have the sense to continue that. At least until he had enough light to avoid wasting even one shot.

His gaze on the dark shapes below, he waited as the dawn light grew stronger and the shapes below began to take on clear definition. Canyon scanned the positions of the men as he prepared to shoot. But the shot that shattered the new dawn didn't come from his Colt. It exploded from the window of the cabin, missing its target. The men dived back into the trees. Two more shots erupted from the cabin and the men stayed inside the tree line.

Canyon cursed silently as he saw all his targets staying under the tree cover. He hadn't expected Jennifer to start shooting. He didn't even know she had a pistol in her things. But daylight was quickly beginning to flood over the land. They'd soon be able to spot him on the roof, he realized grimly. The voice came from the trees, still conciliatory but with an edge of effort in it.

"You're just wasting time, Sam," it called. "Stop shooting and come on out." They were still concentrating on the front of the cabin, and staying flat, Canyon crawled behind the short chimney. He couldn't draw a bead on the men below from where he crouched, but they wouldn't spot him so quickly.

The dawn quickly became day and the morning sun peeked across the top of the hills. Jennifer had apparently decided to stop shooting, and he could only wonder what she was contemplating. He got a glimpse of two of the men hunkered down alongside a black walnut, both waiting, and he noted that neither had a gun in hand. But he hadn't long to wonder about Jennifer's next move as he suddenly heard the creak of the front door being opened. Jennifer's voice came next as she stepped outside.

"You've made a mistake. There's nobody here but me," she said, and Canyon saw the six men leave the trees and move into the open to disappear from his sight.

"Who the hell are you, girlie?" one asked.

"Mary Smith," Jennifer answered.

"Well, you stay right there, Mary Smith, and we'll just see for ourselves," one of the men said. Canyon heard him and at least two of the others stride into the cabin. He still couldn't see Jennifer but he could hear the men inside the cabin. "She's right, there's nobody here," one said, and they hurried back outside. "You a friend of Sam Shell?"

"Never heard of him," Jennifer answered.

"We know he was livin' here," the man said.

"My uncle bought the cabin last month. That's all I know," Jennifer said.

"Maybe he did and maybe he didn't. Maybe you're here waiting for Sam Shell?" the man countered.

"Nonsense," Jennifer snapped. She was holding to her story. More important, she was keeping their attention on her. Canyon slid on his stomach to the edge of the roof and took in the scene below. One man confronted Jennifer, two others standing by. The other three were back farther in a half-circle. It would be the best chance he'd get, maybe the only one. Canyon frowned. He knew they'd gun him down without a second thought if given the chance. He could do no less, and he raised the Colt, took aim.

The man was still arguing with Jennifer. "Maybe we'll just wait here with you a spell, girlie," he said. "We'll see that you don't get lonely."

"There's no need for that. I told you nobody's coming here," Jennifer said.

Canyon's finger tightened on the trigger of the big Colt. He chose the three nearest Jennifer as first, aimed, and fired. His three shots were so fast they sounded almost as one as he moved the Colt a fraction of an inch between each shot. The three men appeared to go into some strange ritual dance, almost as though they were Indian dancers bending and stomping, before they collapsed. The other three men froze for an instant, unsure where the shots had come from, and Jennifer's scream rent the air over the shots as she dived to the ground. But Canyon was firing again and the fourth man spun around and fell.

The last two had finally pinpointed where the shots were coming from. One raised his gun to fire, but he never got his shot off as Canyon's bullet slammed into him and he doubled up as he fell. The last man had spun and was in a half-dive, half-run to the tree line. He reached it as Canyon's last bullet sent splinters of bark from an alder inches from his diving figure.

"Damn," Canyon swore as he reloaded and lost precious seconds doing so. Finished, he holstered the Colt and gripped the edge of the roof with both hands. He swung himself over, hung for a moment, and then dropped to the ground to land on the balls of his feet. He saw Jennifer lift her head from where she lay on the ground and stare at him, her mouth dropping open.

"Good morning," he called out to her as he ran past, Colt in hand again. But the last man had reached his horse in the trees and was racing away through the woods. Canyon halted at the tree line and turned back, dropped the six-gun into its holster, and walked toward Jennifer, who had pushed to her feet, her stare of surprise now a glare.

"You were up there all the time, weren't you?" she hissed.

"I was, ye of little faith."

"Little faith? What else was I to think?"

"Pure thoughts, lass, such as that I wouldn't desert you."

"It was a natural reaction." Jennifer frowned, but her tone had lost its strength. "Besides, you should've told me," she said, flaring again.

"I didn't want to wake you." He smiled. "It was a last-minute decision."

Her light-blue eyes narrowed at him. "Hah!" she

sniffed. "You can talk about little faith. I'll talk about not believing in anyone."

He shrugged and tossed her a conciliatory smile. "No matter," he said. "Get your things together and we'll be leaving here. Certain things are clear enough now."

"Such as?" She frowned as she followed him into the cabin.

"It seems damn clear now that your pa lit out because he expected visitors."

"You can't say that for sure."

"Sure enough for me," Canyon said. He watched her lips grow tight as she looked away. Even if she really knew nothing, she realized the truth of his words. Of course, she'd not admit it, but he saw the concern behind the stubbornness in her eyes. "It'll be damn hard, but I'll try to pick up a trail to follow."

"It'll be impossible," Jennifer said.

"Maybe. I'm pretty good, but I'm no trailsman. I'm not just tossing in the towel here, though."

Jennifer tossed him a sidelong glance. "That sounds like something I ought to be saying," she remarked.

"Meaning what? You're paying me to help you find him, aren't you?"

"Yes, but it seems to me you're interested above and beyond the call of duty," she said.

He paused before answering while his mind raced to find the right words, and he cursed her acuity and her suspiciousness. "You're right," he said, and allowed a trace of sheepishness to come into his voice. "It's not just the money. I've come to care about your searching and what it has to be doing to you. You've got to be churning inside with worry and uncertainty. I guess it's gotten to me. You've gotten to me."

Jennifer listened, blinked at him, and he saw the anxiousness to believe and be comforted rise up inside her. "Thank you," she said softly. "I didn't think you really understood. One more side of Canyon O'Grady."

"There are lots more." He laughed, and she nodded, took a step forward, and her lips came up to touch his mouth, a quick, delicate kiss, and then she pulled away.

"Thank you for caring," she said. "Maybe you won't have to try to pick up a trail." Canyon's eyes questioned as he waited. "There's an elderly couple, Todd and Mary Dunne. Pa's been friends with them all his life. They were the only ones he regularly kept in touch with over the years. If he were really in trouble, chances are he might go to Todd and Mary as a last resort."

"Where are they?" Canyon asked, his interest quickening at once.

"South, across the border in Tennessee, near a place called Standing Stone," Jennifer said. "They have a house there."

"Let's ride. It'll be two days at least, maybe three," Canyon said.

Jennifer nodded and hurried into the cabin to gather her things. He climbed back onto the roof, retrieved his bedroll, and had the palomino ready and waiting when she came outside again. She stepped past the slain figures with her eyes straight ahead, climbed onto her horse, and still refused to glance at them. Only when he began to lead the way into the woods did she speak.

"Shouldn't we have done something back there?" she asked.

"Such as a proper Christian burial?" he asked, and she nodded solemnly. "On a spiritual level, I'll confess my sin next time I get to church. On a practical level, they'd have left us for the buzzards, so I'm just paying in kind.''

She thought for a moment, accepted the answer in silence, and concentrated on her riding as he sent the palomino into a fast canter downhill.

He kept a hard pace through the day, and when night fell and he found a spot to camp, Jennifer fell asleep the minute she finished her supper of beef strips.

Canyon lay awake only a little longer and thought about Jennifer as she breathed in steady sleep nearby, the loose nightgown rising and falling with the curve of her breasts. Finding her pa alive could well be a mixed blessing for her. There'd be other pains she'd have to wrestle with then, he was almost certain of that with each passing day. He let a sigh escape him, turned his flame-red hair to one side in the bedroll, and found himself thinking of Coleridge's words: ''In today, already walks tomorrow.''

6

O'Grady set a slower pace the next day as the air grew warm and heavy. They rode due south until, in mid-afternoon, they crossed the Cumberland River at one of its wiggly curves. They rode into a thick stand of forest land where small offshoots of the Cumberland ran in all directions, some joining with water from strong, underground springs.

It was almost dusk when he halted beside one of the rivers that ran with clear, cool abandon down a dip in the land.

"I'd like to stop and bathe," Jennifer said, and Canyon's eyes surveyed the section of the narrow river, hardly more than a wide stream, that coursed before them.

"Guess there's no reason not to," he said. "We'll have to make camp for the night soon. This might be as good a spot as any."

"I don't want an audience," she said as he dismounted at the water's edge.

"You want me to chase away every beaver, raccoon, woodchuck, and owl in these parts?" Canyon frowned.

"Very funny! Just any creatures with red hair."

"Now, that's asking for a terrible lot of self-discipline, lass," Canyon said. "Self-discipline is something I've always had a problem with."

"I'm giving you a chance to work on it. You can thank me later for that."

"I'll go along with you, but you'll not be getting any thanks for it," Canyon muttered. He strolled to where a dense cluster of shagbark hickory grew tall and thick in the moist soil it favored. He went into the trees and the brush that effectively screened the river from him, and sat down against the scaly gray bark of one of the trees. He put his head back, closed his eyes, and relaxed as he heard the sounds of her in the water. Not more than five minutes had gone by when her scream pierced the air; he leapt to his feet and charged out of the brush.

She was nowhere in sight and then he heard her scream again, downstream, and he spun and leapt onto the palomino. He sent the horse charging along the edge of the bank. Jennifer's scream came again and then he spotted her, a dozen yards ahead.

She was in the middle of the river, which had suddenly changed character, the water flecked with swirls of white foam and flowing a hundred times faster than it had above. He cursed silently. She was clinging to the smooth top of a rock with both hands, but she was already slipping away.

He raced Cormac along the shoreline. It wasn't hard to put together what had happened. He'd seen it happen before, the quietness of the river a deception, nothing but a short stretch of placidness and in the center a tremendous, subsurface current that rushed toward white water. Jennifer had unwittingly ventured out into the center and been swept downstream instantly, the white water quick to appear a few dozen yards below.

Canyon swore again as he saw Jennifer's hands slip from the rock and with a sharp cry she was swept along in the water, which quickly grew more tumultous.

Spray whipped over more rocks as they appeared and Canyon watched Jennifer fight a losing battle against the turbulence and pull of the water. She tried to swim, to fight against the rush of the water that turned her one way and then another, but her arms only flailed wildly. He saw the panic in her face. There was a waterfall somewhere downriver, but that wasn't the real danger. Jennifer would be dashed to death against the rocks long before she reached the waterfall. Even as he watched, she was slammed hard into a rock and he heard her gasp of pain. She made another grasp at one of the rocks, clung for perhaps a dozen seconds before being swept away again.

Canyon sent the palomino racing beyond where Jennifer struggled in the water. He kept Cormac running hard as he scanned the roaring, white-foamed rapids. He'd barely be able to swim in it alone, he realized. He'd never negotiate it with Jennifer, and a quick glance back at her told him she was weakening fast. He sent the palomino racing on still farther ahead until, with another quick glance back at Jennifer, he skidded to a halt, leapt from the horse, and took his lariat from the strap. Working with feverish haste, he wrapped the rope around the trunk of a slender black walnut, secured it to the tree with two knots, and peered back at Jennifer once more. He'd time to shed boots and shirt, he saw, and he did so before he plunged into the racing water, the lariat in one hand.

He felt the tremendous pull of the water at once as he started to swim across it and was immediately taken downstream. But instead of wasting energy trying to fight the tremendous current, he went downstream with it as he also maneuvered farther in the center of the rapids. He turned, fought to move a little farther into midstream, and saw Jennifer being swept toward him. It was too dangerous to try to catch her. He could easily miss, and a miss would spell her doom. He'd never be able to overtake her, he knew, and still holding on to the end of the lariat, he saw her tumbling, turning toward him, almost abreast of him now. He counted off another ten seconds and then pulled the lariat tight.

Jennifer came hard against it, taking the center of the stretched rope forward with her, and Canyon used all his strength to swim across and upward, bring the lariat in a circle around her. He took another turn around her as he let the water sweep him toward her, and then, the rope securely tied around her, he struck out for the shore. Again, he didn't try to fight the roaring current but let it take him downriver as he crossed the water at an angle, clinging to the rope that held Jennifer.

Finally, Jennifer almost at his side, he was swept onto the shore; he dug his feet into the soft soil of the bank and pulled hard on the lariat. He swung Jennifer against the shore as he stumbled forward and pulled her from the last clutching watery hands of the rapids. She was only barely conscious as he hauled her farther up on the mossy bank, turned her on her stomach, and pressed hard against her ribs. She coughed up a mouthful of water, groaned, and snapped into consciousness as she drew in deep, gasping breaths. For the first time, he became consciously aware of her nakedness; her slender body, long waist, and long legs; a beautifully rounded rear; her milk-white skin glistening with little droplets of water. She half-turned to him, crossed arms over her breasts, and kept the lower part of her torso toward the ground.

He rose before she said anything, strode to Cormack, and took a rain slicker from his saddlebag. He tossed it to her and watched her disappear inside it and then sit up. "Than you, Canyon," she murmured. "It all happened so suddenly."

"Not your fault. One of those things." He reached a hand out to her. "Can you ride?" he asked. She nodded and took his hand as he pulled her to her feet. He sat her in front of him on the palomino and rode back upriver to where they had halted at the calm water. She slid from the saddle and hurried to take a towel from her saddlebag. He tethered Cormac while, still under the rain slicker, Jennifer dried herself and retrieved her clothes from the bank. She stepped behind a tree to dress and reappeared moments later as Canyon set a small fire while the darkness moved in. He set out his bedroll and relaxed on it.

Jennifer came to sit close beside him as he warmed some strips of dried beef, and she ate in silence. Only when the meal was over did she find her tongue. "Seems I can't do anything right."

"It could've happened to anybody," Canyon said. "The current grabs at you like a giant, unseen hand."

"Maybe if I'd reacted faster."

He smiled back. "Reactions are built into us, slow, fast, calm, excitable, whatever. They go too far back to suddenly change, be it survival or modesty," he added.

Jennifer's slow smile held admission and something else. "Some things can be changed," she said, half-turned, and came toward him. "You said you cared about me, and you've proved it again. It's time I did some proving."

As he watched, she began to unbutton the shirt, her long, thin fingers working slowly, unclasping the first button, then the second, and the third and last followed. She wriggled her shoulders and the shirt fell away. Canyon gazed at the softly sweeping curve of her breasts, each milk-white mound topped with a small, delicately pink nipple centered on an equally delicate pink areola. With a quick motion she undid the riding skirt, slid it down along with her bloomers to stand proudly naked in front of him. Her long, narrow waist flared to nicely balanced hips, a flat abdomen, and a slightly curved belly that swept down to a triangle of jet-black, tangled curliness. She had long, smooth legs, which were perhaps a trifle thin yet lovely enough, and she stood very still, a quiet pride in her eyes as she watched him gaze at her with a mixture of enjoyment and surprise.

A soft, warm breeze blew and her jet-black tresses moved gently.

Canyon's smile was pure appreciation. "Beautiful," he murmured. "But you should be standing on a giant seashell." Jennifer's frown questioned and he went on. "The great Renaissance painter, Botticelli, painted the goddess Venus being born out of the sea standing on half a giant shell, delicate, pale white, just as you are. Even her hair blew gently as yours on a warm breeze sent by two wind gods."

"Something more you learned with the good friars?"

"Indeed. Beauty, art, and culture were never neglected. Man does not live by bread alone," Canyon replied as he reached out and curled his hand around the full cup of one lovely breast and felt the satin-smooth warmth of her. He pulled gently and she came forward, her hands finding his shirt, pulling buttons open while he shed his gun belt, pushed down trousers, and felt his shirt come off in her hands.

Jennifer instantly pressed herself against him and he heard his own gasp of pleasure at the deliciousness of her touch, skin to skin, body to body, the touching that was more than touching, all the tactile senses rising, flowing into one another, pulsating messages, prologue of passions. He felt the soft-wire tendrils of her curly nap against his groin. His hands came down to clasp both halves of her smooth, round rear, and Jennifer gasped out.

He gently lowered her to the bedroll and again he let his eyes drink in the long-waisted loveliness of her slender legs pulled halfway up, turned slightly away, and held tight together. But her lips were parted and waiting, her long-curved breasts sweeping upward, the tiny, delicately pink tips almost quivering. He brought his body half over hers again and felt the softness of one breast against his chest, the nipple gently firm. He cupped his hand around its sweet fullness and Jennifer gasped out again. She pulled his face down to hers, his mouth onto her own lips as they opened wide for him, her tongue swiftly circling, darting, sliding, thrusting forward and pulled back to thrust deep into his mouth again.

Canyon brought his mouth slowly down along her throat, his tongue moving in a slipping path across her collarbone, and he felt her hands tighten against him as he lapped a gentle path down over her breasts, chose one, and closed his lips over it.

"Oh, oh, my God," Jennifer cried out even as her fingers dug into his shoulder. "Oh, Canyon . . . oh, oh, my." He circled the pink tip with his tongue, the tiny ridges of flesh that lay around the outer edge of the areola, and gently drew her breast deeper into his mouth. "Ah . . . aaaaah, oh, yes, yes, oh, God," Jennifer cried out, but her hands made tiny pushing motions against his shoulder and he slowly brought his mouth away. "No, no," she gasped out instantly, and pulled his face down to her breasts, cradling him between their soft sweeping curves, bringing one pink tip to his lips with a murmur of wanting, and he drew her in again.

She uttered a long low sigh and he let one hand gently trace caressing, invisible lines across her abdomen, then down to touch the tiny indentation in the center of her slightly convex belly. He moved his hand across to first one hip, then the other, and then, slowly, ever so slowly, down to the dense, curly triangle, pushing his fingers through the brush of it. He pressed down gently on the pubic mound.

Jennifer groaned, and the groan became another kind of sound: panic and desire mixed together as his hand closed over the dark and secret places where warm moistness had already come to welcome, to prepare the path of pleasure. He touched the lips that knew no word but ecstasy, and Jennifer cried out, long low cries, more breath than sound, and her slender legs parted, falling open as a flower's petals open to the sun.

He paused to enjoy the loveliness of her long-waisted, slender body, the milk-white skin that seemed absolutely pure in the firelight's glow. Her arms slid around his neck and she turned herself to him as she made small, half-moaning sounds. He brought himself over her and his pulsating warmth came against the dense, curly nap.

Jennifer's soft cries turned to a sharp half-scream of delight and desire. Her hands dug hard into his shoulder blades and she held herself almost still, poised, the waiting made of that special anticipation that only the flesh can bring. He came completely over her, brought the throbbingness to her, touched, paused, touched deeper, yet held at the very threshhold.

"Oh, Canyon . . . oh, oh . . . oh, yes, yes, take . . . take me," Jennifer begged, her words gasped out, each a rush of breath. He let himself go forward into the smooth, lubricious pathway, and her scream rose upward, a cry of delicious fulfillment. He saw the long-curved breasts fall from side to side as Jennifer's body twisted one way and then the other.

He thrust forward deeply, fully into the wet, warm tunnel. Flesh slid against flesh, sensations erupted, contained, yet exploding beyond all else; her womanness surrounded him as he moved back and forward, thrust and drew back, rotated within the sweet confines.

Jennifer's voice rose into the night with one scream of delight upon the other. She clutched at his shoulders, her arms reaching out to encircle his neck and bring his face down into the soft, sweet valley between her breasts. He let himself press into her breasts, his lips moving from one to the other, rolling between each and somehow embracing both as he continued to thrust deep inside her.

"Canyon," he heard Jennifer gasp, sudden urgency in the short cry. Her slender legs fell open and closed hard to slap against his side, staying there, pressing harder as her hips lifted, surged forward. He saw her jet-black hair fly from side to side as she tossed her head, and her eyes were open, staring at him with something between apprehension and anticipation. "Oh, oh, oh, God . . . oh, I'm . . . I'm coming . . . oh, oh, Canyon," Jennifer cried out, each word more intense than the one before until she was screaming the words and her long-waisted form quivered under him.

"Now, now oooooh, now, now, now," Jennifer screamed, and Canyon felt her passion contract around him. He let himself explode with her and the night stood still, the world suspended in time and ecstasy.

Finally, with little quivering sounds made of pure protest, Jennifer lay back on the bedroll, and only when she sighed did the satisfaction of passion consummated come into her voice. She lay still for a long moment and then turned to him and came into his arms. One slender leg rose to come over his thigh. Her hand caressed his chest and her lips touched his in a soft, quick kiss. "It was wonderful, Canyon," she murmured, and she stretched herself languorously, a sensuous, feline motion, reveling in the way his eyes admired the beauty of her body, the lovely, sweeping curves of her milk-white breasts.

"It was," Canyon agreed.

"Did the good friars teach you about that, too?" she asked, a sly smile edging her lips.

He returned the smile. "No, my teachers in that were more interested in pleasure than penance."

"They taught well," Jennifer said. Her hand came up to move along his chest, tracing tiny, tentative paths as she pulled herself up close to him until she rested one breast against his cheek. "Love me again, Canyon," she murmured, and brought one delicate pink tip to his lips, pushing ever so gently.

His lips opened, drawing her into his mouth as she cried out in delight. Her hand moved across his muscled frame, the tentativeness gone from it, hurrying downward to clasp around the warm maleness already beginning to respond. "Oh, God," Jennifer gasped at his touch, and an instant intensity swept over her. She pressed herself against him and her hand clasped, stroked, explored. With each motion she cried a tiny gasp of pleasure.

He felt himself grow quickly for her, flesh answering flesh, words made of the tactile senses, words beyond denying, and Canyon rolled atop her and felt the long, slender legs open to come together around him.

"Sweet vise," he murmured to her.

Jennifer surged her body upward, seeking, searching to encompass all of him, and drew into her self that pinnacle of pleasure.

"Ah, aaaaaah," she groaned as he filled her wanting and two became one, joined in a world of absolute ecstasy, excluding all else in the special world of the utter privacy of passion. Jennifer's cries grew stronger, more insistent, gasped pleasures even greater than the first time, and when her jet-black tresses flew from one side to the other in a dark halo of wildness, she screamed in the moment of moments, that time when there was no time.

She finally drew back, stretched herself on the bedroll, and her long, half-groaned sigh was a hymn to satiated fulfillment. She curled into his arms and was asleep in minutes as he settled down beside her. She turned only once through the rest of the night, and when morning came, Canyon leaned back as she rose, stretched, and used her canteen to wash.

He waited, enjoyed every motion of her body as she began to dress: the smooth suppleness of her waist as she turned; her legs as they moved with slender grace as if she were doing a small, private ballet of her own; the way her breasts swayed and dipped as she bent over, straightened, leaned to one side and then the other. Watching a lovely woman dress was perhaps more enjoyable than watching her undress, Canyon decided. It was more pure appreciation of beauty, unmarred by the distraction of anticipation.

He washed and dressed when she finished, and the new sun had already warmed the morning when they rode out.

He held a steady pace, pausing only to rest the horses. The terrain remained rich forest land with enough open space for good riding. They were still in Kentucky when dark came and he chose a place to bed down. Supper was made of fruits he had found along the way, an untamed orchard of delicious apples, clusters of dark-red wild grapes, and the riches of a raspberry stand.

"We ought to be into Tennessee by tomorrow night," Canyon told Jennifer as she curled against him on the bedroll. A moment of excitement touched her eyes. She lifted her mouth to his and once again turned the night into a time of wild abandon. It was, for her, part wanting and part hiding, he knew, a release and a refuge. He was certainly not going to deny her either. To do so would be ungentlemanly, he reminded himself as he went to sleep.

The next day saw the land grow flatter, the forest stands thinning out. Canyon kept moving southwest, gauging his directions by the sun. It was into the afternoon when he spotted the wagon moving along a narrow road, a high-sided body with round corners and a rounded top, closed on all four sides except for the driver's compartment. It was a merchant's wagon, with pots and pans hanging from hooks along the sides. He turned the palomino to come up across the road as the wagon neared, and he saw a portly figure at the reins, a battered fedora partly covering gray, wispy hair.

"Greetings, friend," Canyon called out. "Is this here Tennessee land we're riding?"

"It is," the man answered.

"Would you know how close we are to Standing Stone?"

"Above five miles the other side of that ridge," the traveling merchant said, and nodded to a low ridge that ran east and west some half-mile or so on.

"Very good. You travel this territory regularly, I take it." Canyon smiled.

"Been doing it for twenty years."

"Would you happen to know Todd and Mary Dunne?" Canyon inquired further.

"I would. They've had a place for longer than I can remember just north of Standing Stone. When you reach the other side of the ridge, take the right-hand road at the giant elm."

"Much obliged," Canyon said. "Good luck to you, friend."

"And to you," the merchant said, snapping the reins over the horse. The wagon rolled on with a tinkling clatter of pots and pans.

Canyon set Cormac into a fast trot and, Jennifer close to him, reached the low ridge and climbed to the top. He spotted the road below and the old elm—indeed a giant of a tree—where it straddled two roads that converged. He saw Jennifer cast an apprehensive glance at the lengthening shadows as she followed him to the road that ran past the big tree. He kept to a fast trot past a line of hop hornbeam and their clustered fruits that lined both sides of the road.

They had ridden perhaps another hour and the first grayness of twilight was beginning to seep down on the land when the square frame house appeared. With surprise Canyon saw Jennifer rein to a halt.

"That might be the place," she said.

"So why are we stopping?"

"I've been thinking," Jennifer said. "Maybe it'd be best if I talked to them alone."

Canyon allowed a small smile to curl inside himself. "You've a good reason for that?"

"Todd and Mary Dunne know me, though I haven't seen them since I was a little girl. If they do know anything about Pa, they'll talk freely to me. They might not with a stranger there."

Canyon let his lips purse as the smile stayed inside. She might be right, he admitted. But maybe she was being more than careful. Maybe trusting went only so far. Perhaps trusting took second place to loyalty, a case of blood being thicker than trust. Or—and he couldn't dismiss the thought entirely—sweet and passionate Jennifer had always known more than she'd let on. Then, with equal possibility, she was becoming increasingly afraid of what she might find out. Whatever the reasons, she was playing a game he could play also, with far more experience.

He sent the smile her way with just the right touch of rueful trust in it. "I guess you'd know best on this, lass. You could be right. I'll wait a little ways up in the trees. You take your time."

He caught the edge of relief in her smile. "I'll be back soon as I can," she said, and sent the brown mare forward.

Canyon watched her go and moved the palomino into the trees as she reached the house, his gaze still fastened on her. He saw her dismount and caught a glimpse of a man opening a door and then Jennifer disappeared into the house.

Canyon slid from the saddle and settled down against the scaly brown bark of a hornbeam. He kept his eyes on the house and saw the lamplight come on as night pushed the dusk aside to envelope the land. Another hour went by before he saw the door open and Jennifer emerge, a man and woman silhouetted in the doorway behind her. She climbed onto her horse, waved back, and as the door closed, rode down the road.

Canyon rose, climbed onto the palomino, and slowly made his way down to the road as Jennifer approached, her eyes searching the trees. "Over here," he called, and she moved toward him.

"They didn't know anything," she said quickly, answering his unasked question. "They haven't seen Pa in years. We had a nice visit with a lot of reminiscing, but nothing more.''

''I suppose you're disappointed,'' Canyon remarked.

''Of course,'' Jennifer said. ''And I don't know where else to look. But mostly I'm terribly tired.''

''I'll find us a spot to bed down,'' Canyon said, and he turned Cormac back into the trees. They rode through the woods, climbed a low hill as the moon filtered its pale light through the trees, and finally halted at a half-circle where two shagbark hickory leaned into each other to form a leafy arch.

Jennifer swung from the saddle and undressed as he set out his bedroll. ''Will you be angry if we don't make love tonight? I'm just too tired, too disappointed, I guess too upset. I feel emptied.''

Canyon's smile was gentle. ''I can understand that, Jennifer, you hoping all this time and now at a dead end.''

She put her arms around him and her lips found his, her kiss longer and stronger than he'd expected. ''Thank you for understanding,'' she murmured when she pulled away.

Canyon undressed and lowered himself to the bedroll. ''But we are going to keep looking, somehow, someway, aren't we?'' he asked.

''Yes, I suppose so, but I don't know how,'' Jennifer answered, not meeting his eyes. She lay down near him but not touching, turned on her side, her back to him. ''Good night, Canyon,'' she said softly—only three words, but he heard the edge of sadness in her voice.

He closed his eyes to welcome sleep as he made a small, silent wager within himself.

7

Canyon let his body and mind sink into a halfway state between being asleep and being awake, suspended between consciousness and unconsciousness. It allowed him a measure of rest while he clung to alertness. Now he half-slept through most of the night and the hour had reached that hanging time before the day appears when the faint sound of movement drifted through to his consciousness. He kept his eyes closed as he became fully awake at once, his ears picking up the rustles of clothes being donned, the softness of careful footsteps.

He listened to the momentary rattle of the bit chains and the creak of stirrup leather. Jennifer was at her horse and he opened his eyes to see her starting to lead the horse behind her. He remained absolutely motionless and watched her move into the trees, pulling her horse slowly after her. Only when she vanished into the darkness did he rise and silently pull on clothes before he hurried to Cormac and also led the palomino after him into the woods. He let his ears become his eyes as he followed the sound of her moving on ahead of him in the forest blackness. Suddenly the sound changed character. She had climbed into the saddle and he quickly did the same while he continued to stay back just far enough to hear her.

Jennifer moved slowly in the dense trees, and suddenly Canyon saw the first grayness of dawn tinge the night. It was followed quickly by another silent surge of gray light, and the dark shredded before his eyes. He glimpsed Jennifer through the trees that took form and shape. He halted instantly and let her ride on as daylight came to his aid. He could see her too plainly. He waited, let her move far enough ahead so she was barely visible before he moved Cormac forward again. She increased her pace through the trees with the help of the morning light. Canyon kept pace with her but was careful to hang back far enough to avoid being spotted by a casual glance she might toss backward.

His lips formed a grim half-smile as he rode. He had won the wager with himself. It had gone exactly as he'd expected it would, and it was a victory that held a sour taste. She had lied about whatever the Dunnes had told her. Did she steal away in the night because of what she had known all along? Or because she was growing more fearful of what she might find out about her father? He pushed aside further speculation as Jennifer reached the end of the thick forest land and rode across a low hill with plenty of open land. Canyon stayed in the trees and let her go out of sight. Only when he was certain she'd gone on far enough did he leave the trees and cross over the hill at a fast canter.

He came in sight of her again as he reached the top of the low hill where, on the other side, the tree cover grew heavier once again. He reined to a halt as he saw Jennifer stop beneath a wide-branched black oak, slide from the saddle, and lower herself against the base of the tree. He watched and, in minutes, saw her left arm fall limply to her side as she slept.

Canyon uttered a silent grunt. She'd probably slept little during the night as she waited for the time to rise and steal away. Now tiredness had forced rest on her. He dismounted and rested against the thin, fissured, gray-brown bark of a box elder. He let himself catnap, welcoming the phases of real sleep in between wakings. He had just snapped awake for the fourth time and the sun was high in the sky when he saw that the figure beneath the branches of the black oak was gone. He climbed onto the palomino, easily picked up Jennifer's tracks, and rode until he came in sight of her again. She had come to an oblong lake and followed the shoreline west. She continued on westward when the lake came to an end, and perhaps another hour had passed when he saw her halt where a tall slab of stone jutted some fifteen feet into the air.

A narrow road led to the right of the stone, and Jennifer swung onto it at once. Canyon followed on the narrow road as it wound through heavily wooded terrain. The sun finally disappeared over the hills.

It was plain that she had received detailed instructions from the Dunnes. The trees on both sides leaned in to make the road even narrower, but suddenly Canyon saw the house, a shack more than a cabin, a lean-to at one side with a lone horse under the slanting roof. Jennifer rode to a halt in front of the shack, had only begun to dismount when the man stepped from the shack, a long-barreled Hawkins in his hands.

Canyon stopped, watched the man halt, drop the rifle as his eyes grew wide, and rush toward the girl. Jennifer met him halfway with a leaping embrace that landed her in his arms.

Canyon heard Jennifer's squeal of excited delight, and he moved forward, leaving the palomino in the trees as father and daughter were still locked in their embrace. He slowed, then hurried forward again, moving in a crouch as Jennifer went into the shack, her father's arm around her. The door was left hanging open as they disappeared inside the shack, and Canyon dropped to one knee as night descended and a lamp was turned on inside the shack.

The trees grew almost to the door of the house, and Canyon, moving on swift, silent steps, darted to the edge of the open door, where he dropped to one knee again. The voices drifted to him with quiet clarity as the dark closed down over the land.

"Alex Koosman killed?" he heard Sam Shell say.

"I was there," Canyon heard Jennifer reply. "I'd learned he was taking a wagon train to Pickett and I went there to meet him. I thought he might've heard from you. I was only hours too late. I knew then that I had to find you. You were the only one left."

"My God," Sam murmured. "All of them dead, all of them murdered. My God."

Canyon half-rose in the new night, moved in a crouch, and dropped to the ground where he could see into the cabin through the open door. He had a good look at Sam Shell for the first time and saw a tall, thin figure, a face that, while lined, did not show its real age, hair still black, and eyes the same blue as Jennifer.

"Why, Pa? What's it all mean?" Jennifer said. "You knew they were going to come after you. That's why you've been running. Why?"

Canyon watched Sam run a hand through his still-profuse hair and suddenly his face had turned old. "It's about something that happened a long time ago. I thought it was buried in the past, never to surface again. But when Rulson was killed and then Akins, I knew something was wrong. That's when I decided to run. It's all like a graveyard opening up, old ghosts coming alive."

"What old ghosts, Pa? You still haven't told me that," Jennifer pressed.

"It doesn't matter. You don't want to know, Jennifer. It's best that way. What matters is what you've told me. If they're as close as you say, it means they've been tracking and trailing, buying information. I can't stay here any longer. I've got to run again," Sam said.

"Who are they? You can tell me that much," Jennifer protested.

Canyon watched Sam Shell draw a deep sigh. "I don't know who they are, Jennifer. That's the gospel truth," the man said. "But yesterday has come alive and I have to run. The less you know about it, the better off you'll be, my child."

"I'll go with you. I can help you run, Pa," Jennifer argued.

"No, no, this is my cross to bear. The past is mine alone to carry. I won't let you become part of it. You've done enough to find your way here to warn me," Sam told his daughter.

Outside, in the darkness, Canyon rose to his feet. He had heard more than enough, and for an instant, the meeting with President Buchanan that had sent him after Sam Shell flashed through his mind. The pieces given him at that meeting were falling into place. He unholstered the big Colt with the ivory grips and moved toward the shack, his lips a thin line. Eavesdropping had told him one thing: Jennifer had never known the truth. Finding out would hurt, and there was nothing he could do to prevent that. He couldn't wait to move in on Sam Shell to spare her feelings. The unexpected could happen, the risk too great. Sam's voice came to him again as he reached the open doorway. "I'm going tonight, Jennifer. I won't wait for morning," the man said.

Canyon moved forward on long strides, stepped through the open doorway and into the shack, the Colt in one hand. "Sorry, there'll be a change in travel plans," he said.

Sam whirled to stare at the big, flame-haired man as shock flooded his long face. "My God, they followed you, Jennifer!"

"Canyon," Jennifer gasped, and Canyon watched Sam's eyes snap to his daughter.

"Jennifer, you know this man?" Sam asked.

"Yes, he's not one of them," Jennifer answered without looking at her father, her eyes on Canyon's unsmiling face. "He was helping me."

"Until you sneaked away without even a kiss goodbye," Canyon said to her while he kept Sam in sight out of the corner of his eye.

"I had to," Jennifer said, a note of apology coming into her voice. "I was going to find you and explain later."

"Now there's no need for that, seeing as how I'm here, big as life," Canyon said brightly.

"Jennifer, what's this all about?" Sam asked.

"This is Canyon O'Grady. He was riding scout for Alex Koosman's wagon train. After the murder, I hired him to help me find you," Jennifer told her father. "I guess if it weren't for the things he's done for me, I wouldn't be here now."

"I'll be thanking you for that, O'Grady," Sam said.

Canyon turned his eyes on the man. "I don't think you'll be thanking me for anything," he said. "The whole name is Canyon O'Grady, United States government agent." He saw Sam's jaw drop open and heard the gasped hiss of astonishment from Jennifer. "You're under arrest," Canyon said coldly.

Jennifer stepped to the side, her eyes peering hard at him, searching the sternness of his face. "My God, it's true, isn't it?" she murmured, shock filling her own lovely face. "You are a government agent."

"Indeed, lass," Canyon said. "Indeed."

Jennifer swallowed hard. "You led me on," she said, anger gathering in her eyes. "You lied to me."

"I didn't lie. I just didn't tell you all of it," Canyon answered.

"Why are you arresting my father?" Jennifer flared. "People are trying to kill him, like they did all the others. He's not out to kill anyone. What's the charge?"

"Robbery and murder," Canyon said, and watched the shock come into her eyes first, quickly followed by disbelief and anger.

"That's preposterous," Jennifer snapped.

Canyon's eyes went to Sam Shell and he saw the emotions race through the man's face at his glance: bitterness, resignation, shame. "You want to tell her or shall I?" Canyon asked, and Sam only stared back in silence. Canyon turned to Jennifer as President Buchanan's words came back to him.

"When the Louisiana Purchase was made, the price agreed on was fifteen million dollars. That was in 1803. The last payment of two million dollars wasn't made until 1807. That shipment was ambushed and attacked, and half a million dollars were stolen. There were seven men involved, though nothing definite could be proven against any of them at the time. The seven men were Don Rulson, Hap Akins, Fred Carrigan, Seth Tanner, Ben Brown and . . ." Canyon paused, shot a glance at Sam Shell. "You want to finish?" he asked.

"Alex Koosman and myself," Sam said, his voice a hoarse whisper.

"Oh, God, Pa," Jennifer gasped as her father averted his eyes from her.

"It was decided at the time that the attack on the shipment could have been carried out as it was only if

105

all or most of the men involved had been working for the government,'' Canyon went on. ''The seven men decided not to try to go near where they had hidden the money until it was absolutely safe. They knew this could be a good while. Now, all of this took place a year before the famous explorer, Meriwether Lewis, was appointed governor of the new Louisiana Territory. Meriwether Lewis had a pretty damn good suspicion of who the seven men were. He knew each and was friends with all.''

Jennifer interrupted to stare at her father. ''Is this all true, Pa? Is it?'' she asked. Sam continued to stare at the floor in silence.

''Meriwether Lewis was a man given to many moods. Apparently after a lot of soul-searching, he decided he couldn't live with his suspicions, indeed his certainties, any longer. He decided to go to Washington to tell officials there what he suspected and name names. He never made it to Washington, did he, Shell?'' Canyon bit out sharply, and saw the man lift his eyes to meet his silent accusation.

''No, he didn't,'' Sam murmured.

''He was murdered at an inn in Tennessee where he'd stopped for the night,'' Canyon bit out as Jennifer, pain filling her light-blue eyes, stared at him. ''It was never clear at the time whether he'd shot himself or been murdered. Some thought one way. Meriwether Lewis was a man whose emotional instability would have let him do that. Others thought not, and now we know they were right, don't we?'' Canyon said, and again turned to Sam Shell.

''If he'd talked, we'd all have been swinging from the gallows,'' Sam burst out, and Canyon heard Jennifer's cry of shock and despair. ''But I didn't do the killing. I'd no part of that.''

''You were there. You were all there. That makes

106

you part of it—an accessory, they call it," Canyon snapped coldly. "You all followed him, saw your chance at that inn, and took it." He turned his eyes to Jennifer again and saw the pain that filled her lovely face as she stared back. "Only, killing Meriwether Lewis didn't work out the way they'd planned. Lewis had left their names in his desk back in Louisiana. Nothing else, just the seven names. But it was enough to make the government decide to keep those seven men under constant surveillance, and that's just what they did, twenty-four hours a day, 365 days a year."

He glanced at Sam Shell, who nodded, suddenly a very old man. "Yes, they never let up on us, somebody always watching, always there. It was terrible, and we agreed we'd quit government work. But that didn't make much difference. They kept watching, always watching. We were all afraid somebody would make a mistake and we'd end up on the gallows, so we agreed it was better to forget about the money than end up being hung. And that's just what we did. We went our separate ways, stayed in touch as best we could. But we knew they still watched us."

"And none of you ever tried to retrieve the money," Canyon put in.

"That's right. The years rolled on, but we all knew that they might still be watching some of us. We all knew that if they caught one of us, we'd all hang, so none of us ever tried to get to the money. After a while it became a part of our lives we all wanted to forget. The money was there but we'd grown afraid to try to get it. Nobody wanted to take the blame for getting us all hung. All these long years it's been a part of the past, maybe not forgotten, but put aside, buried. And now the ghosts have all come alive. I don't know why. I don't understand it," Sam said, his eyes almost glazed.

"They've come alive because somebody learned about that robbery all those years ago," Jennifer said.

"That's right, and decided to get the money for himself," Canyon added.

"But how'd he learn?" Sam asked. "None of the others would've talked. I know them. Proof is they've been all killed."

"The case of Meriwether Lewis was never officially closed, his death still a question mark. Neither was your robbery. Somebody got hold of the file. I'd guess somebody who once worked for the government, just as you seven had. He first had to be sure nobody went for the money—and none of you talked, not even in a deathbed confession—so he set out to silence each of you except one. He's done that now, and that leaves you, the one he figures to make tell him where you hid the half-million."

"Where do you fit in, O'Grady?" Sam asked.

"The Treasury Department still kept a finger on the case over all these years. I told you, the file was never closed. Somebody learned that most of you involved were suddenly being killed. When the fifth man, Ben Brown, was killed, I was called in. I decided to get to Alex Koosman first. But they killed him under my nose."

"And you've no idea who's doing it, who's after me?" Sam asked.

"No idea," Canyon said. "But he's planned damn well, hired teams of killers to do what he wanted done, scouted well, and come up with solid leads. The sooner I take you in, the safer I'll feel."

"If he catches me, I'll talk," Sam said. "I won't die for that money. I wouldn't all those years ago. I won't now."

"But you will now. Soon as you tell him what he

wants to know, you'll be killed just like the others were," Canyon said.

"My God!" Jennifer cried out.

"No matter now. I'm taking you in, Sam Shell," Canyon said. "We'll stay here for the night." He picked up the man's rifle, emptied the shells from it, and put it in a corner of the shack.

"Give Jennifer the cot," Sam said, and Canyon nodded, went back to the doorway, and gave a long, sharp whistle. Cormac appeared in moments and trotted to the door of the cabin. Canyon took the lariat from where it hung on the fork swell of the saddle, holstered the Colt, and returned inside the shack.

"You first," he said to the man. "That corner over there ought to do fine."

"Just fine," Jennifer's father grunted bitterly as Canyon bound his wrists and ankles and tied the other end of the rope to the leg of a puncheon table.

"May I go outside and get my things?" Jennifer asked, and he nodded. He followed her out of the shack, watched as she took the loose blue nightgown from her saddlebag, and stepped behind one of the nearby trees. She came out when she'd changed, her eyes peering hard at him. "Is all this tying up necessary?" she asked.

"You have a way of running off in the night. I wouldn't want you taking anyone with you," Canyon said blandly.

"It was all a lie, I see that now, all the talk about caring, wanting to really help, all of it lies," Jennifer said. "Oh, you saved my life, but only because you needed me to lead you to Pa. Making love to me was just another lie, to make me care for you, trust you."

"There's truth that is a lie, and there are lies that are truth. You'll have to make your own separations," Canyon said.

"How?" she tossed back angrily.

"Use your heart, not your head. Listen to your instincts. Feel instead of think," he said with a kind of gentle gruffness.

"But you're still going to tie me up," she said grimly.

"I'm just using my instincts." He grinned at her and followed her into the shack. He tied her wrists and a loose lead rope to the end of the cot, giving her plenty of slack to turn and move about. He'd hear anything else, he was certain, and he stretched his bedroll in the doorway, half outside the shack. Jennifer was exhausted, he knew, and he listened until she was asleep before he closed his eyes. During the night, he woke twice as she tossed; he cast a glance at Sam Shell and saw the man hard asleep.

The night passed quietly otherwise and Canyon woke with the dawn. He was dressed when Jennifer woke, then Sam Shell, and he untied them both and let them wash and dress. "Get your things," he said to the man finally. "I won't tie you while you ride. Don't try anything stupid. I want to take you in alive."

"We wouldn't dream of spoiling your plans," Jennifer snapped.

"Now, Jennifer, the man's only doing his job," Sam said to her.

"Exactly," Canyon agreed with a smile. "And he's not put off by sweet reasonability."

Sam allowed a small shrug. "Can't blame a man for trying," he said. "I figure I'm dammed either way now. If I'm caught by whoever's after me, I'll be killed soon as I talk, according to you. And when you bring me in, I'll be hung."

"You've got some kind of chance if I bring you in," Canyon said. "A judge or a jury might buy your story about not doing the killing and keep you off the gallows.''

"That's a maybe, and a slim one," the man said.

"It is," Canyon conceded. "But there's no maybe about the other way." He walked to Cormack and climbed onto the palomino. "Let's ride," he said. Jennifer pulled herself onto the brown mare, her face set. She still was a lovely figure of a woman. "You ride beside me, Jennifer," he said. "You ride a half-dozen paces back," he ordered her father as he began to move through the trees.

"You'll make better time on the road," Sam remarked from behind.

"And it'll be easier to see us on the road," Canyon answered.

"You think they're that close?" Jennifer's father said, alarm quick in his voice.

"Wouldn't bet against it," Canyon said. "Whoever's after you has inside and outside information. He's had men close on our tail all along. I'll take as few chances as I can till I turn you over to a federal marshal."

"When will that be?" Sam asked.

"Another day or two. There's a marshal's station at Acorn Juncture. Marshal George Bundy is supposed to wait there for word from me. He'll get more than just word, now," Canyon said.

"What's the difference between you and a federal marshal?" Jennifer asked.

"A federal marshal arrests people and brings them in. Sometimes he just takes in people others have arrested. Sometimes he does some law-keeping. Mostly, though, he's the arresting arm of the federal government. A government agent tracks down trouble and troublemakers anywhere and everywhere. Federal marshals have a territory. I go anywhere a trail takes me.''

"And do anything you please," Jennifer snapped.

"Pretty much." Canyon smiled. He broke off further talk by sending Cormac into a fast trot. They followed the nearby road to its end, staying in the trees as long as they could, and then took open land across a series of low hills. They rested at midday by a stream, letting the horses drink.

Sam Shell sat alone, consumed with his own thoughts. The man was reviewing his life haunted by one event so many years ago, Canyon wagered silently. He could almost feel sorry for Shell until he thought of a brilliant explorer and pioneer named Meriwether Lewis. Maybe Shell hadn't done the actual killing, but he was stained with the blood of it. Chickens have a way of coming home to roost, Canyon mused silently.

O'Grady set a hard pace for the rest of the day, then found a spot to bed down near a deep gorge that looked over the distant Cumberland River. He'd found a stand of wild fruits that served as supper, but Jennifer was almost too tired to eat. He let her wash and change and then tied her father again, this time to the base of a slender black walnut.

Jennifer turned to him as he approached her, kept her voice to a low murmur. "You enjoyed having me," she said. "You could enjoy it again, as often as you liked."

"All I have to do is let him go." Canyon smiled, and her silence answered, her eyes searching his. Her breasts just touched the loose nightgown with two tiny points, promises of the treasures concealed within. "I'll take the first part of the offer, but not the second," he answered, and saw her lips tighten.

"The hell you will," she said, and spun away from him.

He reached out and caught her arm. "You're forgetting something," he said, and raised a length of the lariat to her. "I'm going to let you share the bedroll. It'll be more comfortable for you."

"I don't want any favors from you, Canyon O'Grady," she said, and he heard the catch in her voice.

"No favors, then, just my way of keeping an eye on you," he said. Canyon took the bedroll to the other side of the campsite, undressed, and tied one of Jennifer's wrists to his. He left enough slack in the rope for her to turn her back to him as they lay down.

"I hate you, Canyon O'Grady," she muttered.

"You make the words of the ancient Greek sage, Chilo, come alive," Canyon said. " 'Love him so, as if you were one day to hate him, and hate him so, as if you were one day to love him.' "

She said nothing more, but before he dropped off to sleep, he heard her stifled sobs and felt sorry for her. But then the innocent always hurt the most, he reflected as he went to sleep.

When morning came, he set a steady pace, Jennifer alongside him again, Sam riding behind. He kept his ears tuned for the slightest sound from the man as they drew closer to Acorn Juncture, but Sam rode with his head bowed, a man seemingly with no heart to flee or fight any longer.

Acorn Juncture, when they reached it a little after midday, was a crossroads set in the middle of nowhere with a long, thin hut that looked more like an outhouse than a cabin. The words FEDERAL MARSHAL'S STATION were painted on a modest sign against the front wall, and a mail-drop box rested alongside the words.

A man stepped from the thin hut, somewhat portly

113

in build, with narrow eyes in a round face. He wore a checked shirt over Levi's, and his gun belt carried a Smith & Wesson seven-shot, rim-fire single-action revolver.

"I'm looking for George Bundy," Canyon said.

"You found him," the man answered, his eyes taking in Jennifer and her father.

"You've something to prove you're George Bundy?" Canyon asked.

"All you need, mister," the man said, reached into the pocket of his shirt, and took out a marshal's badge. He hung it onto his shirt with an almost apologetic half-smile. "I don't always wear it. Brings too many headaches." He pulled a small square of folded paper from another pocket and handed it forward.

Canyon took it and quickly scanned the words engraved in fine, ornate script.

Be It Known That
George Bundy
Is Duly Sworn In and Appointed
United States Marshal
This Day of June 7, 1853

Canyon took in the seal at the bottom, imprinted on the paper so as to be beyond forging, folded the credentials, and handed them back to George Bundy. "Agent Canyon O'Grady," he said with a smile. "I've a prisoner for you, Sam Shell."

George Bundy's narrow eyes widened more than Canyon had thought possible. "I'll be dammed," he said. "I'd orders to wait here for word from you. I didn't think it'd be this." His eyes went to Sam Shell again for a moment. "So you tracked him down. Damn good work, I'd say," the marshal remarked.

"He's all yours now," Canyon said. "I'll make my

report to Washington when I get back. I'd bring him to a safe jailhouse soon as you can. Somebody else wants to get hold of him.''

"Don't you worry about that. I'll take him straight to Ladentown. There's a prison van there. We'll take him the rest of the way in it with three guards riding shotgun. I'll put him in irons for now," George Bundy said.

Jennifer's voice interrupted. "I'm going with my pa," she said, and drew a frown of surprise from the marshal.

"Jennifer Shell, his daughter," Canyon explained. He turned to the young woman. "You can't do that, Jennifer," he said. "The marshal's not running a wet-nurse service. You can go to Washington and meet your pa there."

"I'm going with him. It's my right," Jennifer insisted.

"I don't know about right, but it'll do no good, not for him and not for you," Canyon told her quietly. "Don't do it. I'll take you back with me if you want."

"No. If I can't ride along, I'll follow," Jennifer said, her chin thrusting forward stubbornly, pale-blue eyes still circled with pain.

"She can ride along," George Bundy cut in. "It won't bother me any and he'll stay in irons." He turned to Jennifer and his narrow eyes grew hard. "But you do one wrong thing, girl, and you'll be in irons, too, understand?"

"Yes, I just want to go with him," Jennifer said.

The marshal nodded, stepped into the hut, and returned with the manacles.

As he put them on Sam Shell's wrists, Canyon drew Jennifer aside. "You've no need to do this. Blindness shouldn't be part of loyalty," he said. "You're only making the hurt deeper by this. I'll see that you get to

Washington. Nothing's going to happen so quickly now. Come with me.''

Jennifer's pale-blue eyes held only the rigidness of pain and anger. ''Not long ago I'd have said yes. But not now, not anymore,'' she replied.

''Then there's no more I'll say now, except Godspeed to you, Jennifer. You're as wrongheaded as you are lovely.'' Canyon turned and strode over to where Bundy had just finished manacling Shell. ''I'll be going on, now, northeast, work my way back to Washington. I'll make a full report there.''

''I'm heading west to Ladentown to pick up the prison van. Then we'll circle back northeast. Maybe I'll see you in Washington. Good luck to you, O'Grady,'' Bundy said.

''And to you, Marshal,'' Canyon said with a nod, and he turned the palomino in a half-circle. He glanced at Jennifer. She sat quietly on her horse and refused to glance back. He flicked the reins and Cormac moved away at a trot. Canyon quickly turned northeast across a low hill. It had gone well enough, he reflected. Any successful case was a good one, but some carried more pain than others. Jennifer was the only real casualty and time would heal her wounds. She'd grow to understand, he felt certain. And perhaps have fond memories of some parts of it, he smiled.

He put further thoughts of Sam Shell from his mind and lifted his clear tenor voice in an old Galway tune. A man and a woman passing in a surrey halted to watch the tall, straight flame-haired figure riding across the tall grass on the magnificent pale-bronze palomino, and they listened to the voice that drifted back to them, firm, jaunty, a smile wrapped in a lilt.

> ''As I rode out to Galway City
> at the hour of twelve at night,

Who should I see but a handsome damsel,
   combing her hair by candlelight.
Lassie, I have come a-courtin',
   Your fine favors for to win,
And if you'll but smile at me,
   Next Sunday night I'll call again. . . ."

As he passed over the hilltop and disappeared down
the other side, the couple moved their wagon on and
tried to remember the tune and the words. That they'd
remember the flame-haired man who rode like a fiery
wind they'd not the slightest doubt.

8

Night had come when Canyon reached the town; he passed a big dead-axle dray loaded with empty beer kegs as he rode slowly down the single street. A sign stuck in the ground a dozen yards from the entrance to town had read PINEY FLATS, and the place seemed little different from a thousand others he had seen. These towns sprang up in unexpected places, like mushrooms, and many just as short-lived. But hunger gnawed at Canyon's stomach and his parched throat cried out in thirst. He saw a square of light stab out into the street from the saloon, reined to a halt in front of it, and tethered the palomino to the hitching post.

PINEY FLATS PALACE, the sign read over his head as he pushed the double doors open and stepped inside a large room, moderately crowded, with an old, nicked bar at one side. There were no more than a handful of waitresses in tight dresses moving among the tables. Piney Flats Palace was definitely a saloon first and a dance hall second.

Canyon halted at the bar, a man with a square face and gray-brown hair behind it. "Can a man get something to eat here?" he asked.

"Buffalo steak," the bartender said.

"That'll do fine," Canyon said. "And some good whiskey?"

"Got some Tennessee sippin' whiskey," the bartender said.

"A bargain," Canyon said, and the bartender poured a shot glass of the amber liquid for him.

"Take a table. I'll tell Cookie to get to work," the bartender said. He ducked under the bar and disappeared into a room behind.

Canyon took his glass, sauntered to a table, sat down, sipped the whiskey, then nodded in satisfaction. It was good, no harsh bite to it. He enjoyed another sip as a girl paused beside the table, thin, a sweetness still in her face despite too much powder and paint and a dress too tight.

"Something to go with that drink, handsome?" she asked.

"Got a buffalo steak on order," Canyon said. "And how'd you know my name?"

A little giggle fell from nicely formed, if a trifle thin lips. "It wasn't hard," she said. "It fitted."

"I'd bow if I weren't seated, lass." Canyon nodded and lifted the glass in a toast. "To a woman of rare perception!"

"Whatever that means." The girl shrugged.

"Bring me a refill and I'll explain it to you." Canyon laughed and she moved away with an extra swing of her nice, trim rear. He relaxed, sat back in the chair, and scanned the room again. Three tables held card players; the bar was moderately filled by men with worn clothes and worn faces, cowhands, line trappers, wagon drivers, and some farmers, their boots caked with the dark mud of newly tilled soil. Altogether an ordinary lot, he concluded, though several tables held clusters of fairly boisterous drinkers. A few girls danced slowly with their partners in the center of the room, the music furnished by a weak player piano.

Canyon saw the waitress leave the bar with his drink on a small tray.

He looked away as she threaded her way past the dancers and the others crossing the room when suddenly, as she passed a table a half-dozen yards away, an arm reached out and she was almost yanked from her feet. He caught the movement out of the corner of his eye, brought his gaze to the girl, and saw her on the lap of a man with his back to him. She tried to balance the glass that slid across the small tray as she was held by the man's arm.

"Sit down, doll," he heard the man say, a gruff, raspy voice.

"Let go," the girl said. "The man's waiting for his drink."

The girl half-blocked his view of the man, but Canyon saw his arm sweep out and send the shot glass on the tray spinning into the air, the whiskey flying out in an amber spray.

"Not now he isn't," the gruff voice said and followed with a harsh, guttural laugh. "You're stayin' here with me, baby doll."

The hum of voices in the room had died down to an uncomfortable silence that let Canyon's voice sound with quiet clarity. "I hope you expect to be paying for that drink, laddie," he said.

The silence grew almost absolute as the man pushed the girl to the floor and stood up, a tall, broad-backed figure that slowly turned around. He had a heavy face, a wide brow, and deeply lined cheeks. His mouth twisted to one side in a perpetual grimace, and his eyes were as cold as ice floes. Long, black, stringy hair hung down alongside the face that wore cruelty in its every tight line. He fastened Canyon with a sneer of contempt.

"You say somethin' to me, sonny?" he rasped.

"I said you spilled my drink and I'll be expecting you to pay for it," Canyon repeated almost affably as he sized up the man: powerful shoulders and ham-hock hands, long arms with fists the size of cannon balls.

The man's twisted mouth grew more twisted in a smile that resembled a gargoyle's snarl. "You expect I'll pay for it, do you? Well, you can expect up your ass. Now, what do you think about that?" he said.

"I think that's right poor manners and I think you'll pay," Canyon said, and rose to his feet. The others began to back away with more speed. The man's snarl of a smile stayed and Canyon saw the tiny glints of sadistic anticipation in the ice-floe eyes.

"I could shoot your eyeballs out before you reach your holster, but that's no fun," the man said. "I'm going to beat you into the floor. When I'm finished with you, your face is gonna be as red as your damn hair."

"Then let's move outside," Canyon said. "No point in breaking up the man's place."

"The hell with that. I like breakin' up places and I'm going to like breaking up you."

Canyon's tone took on a sudden biting edge and the calm affableness left his face. "You talk too much to be worth a tinker's damn," he said.

The twisted mouth spit out a roar and the man charged, long arms upraised, just as Canyon expected. He saw the hard, curving left come at him and he moved his head just a fraction of an inch to let the blow miss him. He brought up his own short, right uppercut and landed it flush under the man's jaw. The man's stringy black hair flew outward as his head snapped back and he fell back onto his rump. It was a blow that would have ended the fight with most men, but the man swung himself up to his feet and Canyon saw as much surprise as pain in the cold eyes.

The man came at him again, but less recklessly this time, a long left hook followed by a right cross, and Canyon easily parried both blows. But the man continued to lash out with both fists, mixing his punches from straight jabs to hooks and wild swings. Canyon ducked and parried when suddenly the man dropped low, swung one long arm in a looping arc with more speed than Canyon expected. The blow caught him in the ribs and he winced as he felt the power of the man. He spun away, avoided another looping blow, and crossed a left hook of his own aimed at the man's gut.

But his opponent still had more speed than he appeared to have, and he sucked in his stomach, avoided the blow, and brought both hands down to grab hold of Canyon's arm. He twisted, turned, and Canyon felt himself yanked forward and sideways as one arm came around his neck. The man had too much strength in his arms to push him away, Canyon realized. He let his body sag, drop downward, and the man bent with him at once. With a quick twist of his shoulder and bringing his powerful leg muscles into use, he sent his foe half-flipping over his back. The man's arm came loose from around his neck as he landed on the floor on one knee. Canyon lifted a sizzling left hook that smashed into the man's jaw, and once again the stringy black hair cascaded outward as the man sprawled on the floor on his back.

Canyon went after him, but too quickly, he saw at the last moment. The man's kick caught him in the groin and he doubled over for an instant. The man roared as he regained his feet and charged at the bent-over figure. But the kick hadn't landed squarely, the pain harsh but not the sickening, overwhelming totality it might have been. Canyon saw the charging figure out of his peripheral vision, stayed bent over until the man dived at him. He dropped down at the last split second and felt the thick, powerful body hurtle over him. As the figure landed facedown on the floor, O'Grady straightened, brought his own leg up, and his kick landed alongside the man's head. "A kick for a kick, bucko," he hissed, and heard the man's oath of pain. The man rose, one side of his face streaming blood. He started to turn when Canyon's short right, delivered with all the strength of powerful back and shoulder muscles, sank into the man's abdomen.

The man's breath left him in a harsh gasp and Canyon's swinging left came up to smash into his jaw. The man staggered back, unable to avoid Canyon's roundhouse right that came down on the twisted mouth with the force of a mule's kick. With a shower of red spouting from his face, he went down, twitched, and lay still.

Canyon straightened up, stepped around the unconscious form, and grabbed hold of the back of the man's collar. With one arm, he dragged the figure across the floor, and someone opened the double doors for him to toss the bloodied hulk out into the street. He returned inside the saloon to a round of cheers and applause and found the slender figure waiting at the table as he returned and sat down.

"Thanks." She smiled, the gratefulness real in her eyes.

"I believe I've a buffalo steak waiting," he said.

"Yes, sir," she said, and hurried away.

Canyon's eyes went to the bartender. "Give me plenty of space," he said, and everyone near paid attention.

"You think he'll be back?" The bartender frowned.

"Sure of it. I know his kind. He's not enough of a

man to take a beating fairly. He'll come back shooting. It's in his eyes,'' Canyon said. "Who is he?"

"Never saw him before tonight. He came in and I figured him for trouble right away,'' the bartender said.

Canyon nodded and drew closer to the table as the girl brought his steak along with a baked potato. "Nothing personal, lass, but stay away from me for a while,'' he told her, and she retreated with a small frown. He unholstered the big Colt with the ivory grips and laid it on the table beside his plate. He cut the meat and used his left hand to eat while his eyes stayed focused on the double doors.

Some of the other customers had returned to their drinks at the bar while still others moved to tables against the far wall. Canyon smiled inwardly as he ate the tasty buffalo, cooked in a good sauce. The potato, too, had just the right flavor.

He had just finished the meal, his eyes on the double doors, when they flew open and the figure burst into the saloon, the face dripping blood, the twisted mouth a great gob of red. As Canyon expected, the man had his gun in hand already, no challenge to a fair draw in him, only murderous vengeance. A shot in the back would do just as well for him, Canyon knew, but he'd been prepared for just that. And he'd counted on the moment it took for the man to sweep the room and find his target.

Canyon's hand closed around the Colt on the table, hardly raising the gun as he saw the man find him. He fired, three shots that blended into one sound in the room, and the man shook and shivered in place. Then, with a twisting, almost pirouette motion, he sank to the floor, the gun falling from his lifeless hand. Canyon quietly slid his Colt back into its holster and it was only then that the others realized he'd never left the chair.

"Somebody get Sheriff Watson," the bartender said, and Canyon's eyes went to the man. "Just a formality. The sheriff always likes to be called when there's a shootin'," the bartender said hastily, and sighed with relief at Canyon's nod.

"I'll have that whiskey, now," Canyon said, and the girl brought it in seconds and there was awe in her smile.

"Who are you, mister?" she asked.

"Canyon O'Grady," the big redheaded man said.

"You're something different, I'll say," she breathed.

"Something different," Canyon repeated, and rolled the words in his mind. "I like that, lass." He smiled. His attention shifted to the doors as the man strode into the saloon, the star-shaped badge prominent on his shirtfront. A middle-aged man with a graying crew cut atop a face distinguished by its ordinariness, the sheriff peered at the form on the floor and then looked up at the bartender.

"Sam told me what happened. Who did him in?" he asked, and the bartender nodded toward Canyon, who rose and walked to where the sheriff waited. "You know who this is, mister?" Watson asked.

"Haven't a notion," Canyon said. "Except he was ugly, mean, and thoroughly dislikable."

"Got a flyer in the office with his picture on it. His name's Lee Sanson, wanted for murder, bank robbery, and horse stealin'," Watson said. "There's a reward for him, fifty dollars. Guess it's yours, mister."

"Guess so," Canyon said carefully, unwilling to have to furnish too much personal information.

"Too bad that federal marshal was killed a few nights ago," Watson said. "He could've filled out the reward papers here and now."

Canyon heard the sheriff's words as they revolved in

his head and felt the furrow dig into his brow. "Federal marshal?" he questioned.

"Yep. He passed through here a few days ago, on his way to a marshal's station south of here. Stopped in at the office," Watson said.

"You mean George Bundy?" Canyon asked, his eyes narrowed at the sheriff.

"That's right, that was his name. Nice feller," Sheriff Watson said.

"He wasn't killed. I met with him this morning," Canyon said.

"Not with him you didn't. We found George Bundy in the woods a few days ago, stripped naked of everything he owned. He's still at Seth Crawford's burying parlor. I sent a rider to Ladentown for instructions as to what to do with the body."

Canyon felt the icy chill sliding through his body, still unwilling to face what he suddenly found he might have to face. "This George Bundy, you sure you didn't make a mistake about the man you found stripped naked and dead? Medium-built man, round face with narrow eyes, a few extra pounds around the middle?"

"No mistake. George Bundy spent over an hour with me. Thin-built feller, long face, and a long jaw," Watson said.

"Damn," Canyon bit out, and the coldness inside him had become ice. "Damn, damn, damn." He tossed a silver dollar on the table to pay for the meal and strode toward the doors.

"Wait a minute. Where are you going? Don't you want the reward?" the sheriff called after him.

"The reward I want is out there in George Bundy's clothes," Canyon said as he raced past the sheriff and out into the night. He leapt onto the palomino, yanked the tether loose, and sent the horse into a gallop. Racing out of town, he began to retrace the paths he had used to reach Piney Flats and put the pieces together as he rode.

The man had killed Marshal George Bundy, taken all his credentials, and stripped the body to make identification almost impossible. It was a piece of luck that the marshal had stopped in to see Sheriff Watson or the body would still be unidentified. The killing was another piece of evidence that pointed to someone who had once worked in the government. That's what let him know about the marshal's field station, and he'd gone there to snoop, probe, wait.

Canyon swore at himself in frustrated fury as the pieces fell into place. He had turned Sam Shell over to the man, given him the prize he sought, put it right in his hands. With Jennifer as an added bonus, he swore. Of course, he'd no way of knowing the truth of it then, Canyon realized, and it was partly plain rotten luck. But he still had been duped, taken in, victory exploding in his face. He swore again and thought about the bogus Marshal George Bundy.

"The bastard probably had a hard time believing his luck," Canyon muttered aloud. "But he was cool. He played the hand out without a hitch." No hired hand this time, Canyon was certain. This man had been the brains behind the plan.

Canyon concentrated on riding through the night and finally drew to a halt beneath an alder. He had ridden most all the day and now deep into the night, and exhaustion pulled at him. He had to take a few hours of rest for himself and Cormac. He stretched out on a bed of broom moss, angry at having to waste precious hours and aware that he had no choice. He slept at once and woke only when the morning sun warmed his face.

He washed with water from his canteen and was riding across the low hills before the sun had cleared the horizon. He had to reach the field station first and try to pick up tracks from there.

It was near noon when he reached the hut, dismounted, and searched the ground on all sides. He spotted the hoofprints where they became clear about a half-dozen yards from the hut, three horses riding almost single-file. He swung back onto Cormac and sent the pale-bronze horse after the tracks that remained clear most of the way in good, soft earth. The man had swung north and Canyon reined to a halt as the land became more open and he saw the circle of hoofprints that covered the ground in a profusion of prints. At least six more horses, perhaps eight, he counted, and an unhappy grunt fell from his lips. But he felt no surprise. The man had never worked alone. He had used bands of hired hands, one to kill Alex Koosman, another to hunt Sam Shell, and perhaps others to do other killings. Now he had picked up another band, men who were no doubt waiting for him to arrive though not with the prize in hand.

But Sam Shell and Jennifer would stay alive until the old man revealed where the money had been hidden. He could only hope that Sam Shell remembered his words and realized the truth of them.

Canyon saw where the tracks led from the open circle of footprints; they spread out into a narrow column of riders and turned south again. The trail led toward the Cumberland Mountains. He followed as the day began to slide into dusk and the dusk into night. Perhaps Shell had disregarded his words and was already leading them to where the money had been hidden those long years ago, Canyon mused. And if he was still refusing to talk, they'd give him the night to think about the hopelessness of his position. As darkness blanketed the trail of hoofprints, Canyon continued forward and his nostrils flared as he caught the scent of a wood fire.

He followed his nose and the odor quickly grew stronger. It soon led to flickering firelight through the trees. Canyon moved closer and the light became a small fire set in the center of a double bank of trees. He slid from the palomino and went forward on foot. He tested each step before he pressed down hard, aware that the snap of a twig would bring disaster. The murmur of voices drifted to him and shadows took on shapes. He crept still closer and the shapes took on features. He spotted Jennifer first, her hands tied, seated to one side of the camp, a man standing guard near her. He surveyed the rest of the camp and saw Sam Shell in the center, seated near the fire, still manacled and his ankles bound now also. The fake Marshal Bundy stood near him and Canyon counted eight other men.

"I'm not telling you a damn thing," he heard Sam say.

"You'll talk, old man, or tomorrow morning we'll make you talk," the fake marshal said.

"I'm too old to worry about pain," Sam said. "And the old ticker isn't what it once was. A little pain won't make me talk and a lot might just send me cashing out altogether. You'll never find the money then. Everything you've done won't mean a hill of beans. So you don't scare me, you sidewinder."

The firelight illumined the fake marshal's narrow-eyed face and Canyon caught the confident sneer that touched the man's mouth.

"You'll talk, old man," the fake marshal said. "Because we're not going to do it your way. Come tomorrow morning, you can watch us go to work on your little girl there. First we'll screw her into the ground, everybody getting a chance at her. If you still aren't talking we'll start to fix her so's no man will ever look at her again. You've got the night to think about it.''

''You scum,'' Sam Shell hissed. ''You dirty, stinking piece of scum.''

''Let's get some shut-eye,'' the man said to the others as he turned away from Sam.

Canyon watched as the figures began to settle down for the night, but not before tying Jennifer to the trunk of a tree. He watched until everyone had found a place to sleep, and then he slowly backed away. He'd wait a few hours at least, until everyone was wrapped in sleep, and he silently made his way back to where he'd left Cormac. They plainly didn't expect to be followed and they'd disdained leaving a sentry, but he thought of the fake marshal's words to Sam Shell. The man was cruelly clever. He knew how to use the power of human emotions. Sam was a tough old bird who'd likely stand up to torture for himself. But to see Jennifer ravaged and tortured, his own daughter brutalized before his very eyes, that was another kind of pressure, and one he'd never be able to withstand, Canyon was certain.

With his own lips pulled tight at the thought, Canyon took a sharp hunting knife from inside his saddlebag, stuck it into the tight space between his belt and shirt where he could quickly reach it, and then carefully retraced his steps to the now silent, sleeping camp. He stretched out in the trees and let himself doze for another two hours, and when he woke, the moon was moving across the far reaches of the sky. He hadn't made plans. They had been made for him, dictated by the grim realities in front of him. There was no chance to free Sam Shell. It'd take far too long to cut his bonds loose and there were too many figures too close to him. Jennifer was the only one he'd be able to free, but perhaps that was for the best, Canyon reflected.

Freeing her would deny the fake marshal his chief weapon against Sam. He scanned the sleeping figures again, his eyes pausing at where the horses were tethered, and he wondered if he dared try to free Jennifer's brown mare as well.

"First things first," he whispered to himself, and began to move forward, circling the campsite until he was opposite where Jennifer lay on the ground, the rope around her waist and the tree. He flattened himself and began to crawl forward, halting to listen and look every few minutes. Jennifer was the only one who turned restlessly, sleep a halfway thing with her.

He moved toward her again, staying on his belly. When he reached her, his arm came out and he clapped one hand over her mouth. Her eyes snapped open in fright and softened with instant relief when she saw him. She nodded her understanding and he drew his hand away, pulled the hunting knife from his waist, and began to cut her ankle ropes first, then her wrist ropes. The rope that bound her to the tree was last, and he held her down with one hand as she automatically began to sit up.

She nodded again, turned, and began to crawl with him from the campsite. When they reached the trees, he halted and sat up and she came into his arms, trembled for a moment, and peered into his eyes. "What about Pa?" she whispered, and he shook his head.

"There's no way, not now," he said. She accepted his answer with the disappointment in her eyes. "Keep going straight, slowly and quietly. You'll come to Cormac. Stay there with him."

"Where are you going?" She frowned.

"To see if I can get your horse. It'll help if you've your own horse to ride," he said, and left her abruptly. He stayed in a crouch and circled to where the horses where tethered. Two of the men lay nearby and Canyon crept to the brown mare. There'd be no chance of making off in complete silence with the horse, he realized, and his brow furrowed in thought. "Sound to cover sound," he murmured, and he stole forward between the mare and the horse beside her, untied her reins from the tree branch where she'd been tethered. He dropped to one knee and slapped the nearest horse lightly on the rump. It was enough to send the animal sideways into the next and in moments the entire string was moving, rubbing, pawing the ground, disturbed and noisily restless.

He heard the two men wake, caught a glimpse of them between the horses' legs as they sat up. "Easy, now, quiet down there," the one called.

"Something spooked them, dammit," the other muttered. "Shut up over there," he called, and lay down again.

The horses slowly began to quiet, but they still moved against one another for another few minutes, and as they did, Canyon backed the mare away and let the sound of their restlessness cover the mare's movements through the trees. He was far enough away when the other horses finally grew quiet, and he circled through the trees back to where he'd left the palomino.

Jennifer met him with her eyes round, filled with uncertainty and apprehension. "What now?"

"We get away from here."

"You can't just leave Pa."

"I can't just walk in and take him, either, now, can I?" Canyon said patiently, and her lips tightened.

"No, I guess not," she muttered. "What are we going to do?"

"Wait and see," Canyon said. "Now put that lovely little rear in the saddle, lass." He swung onto Cormac and watched her mount up.

"He'll kill Pa," she said.

"No he won't. That won't get him what he wants," Canyon said. "But he's smart. He'll be quick to put two and two together. He'll know I'm the one who came after him and took you."

"What'll happen then?" Jennifer asked as Canyon led the way up a hillside.

"I don't know. We'll have to watch, wait, try to find a way, and if we can't find a way, we'll try to make one," Canyon said. "Who is this man? Did you learn anything about him while you rode most of the day with him?"

"Yes, everything," Jennifer said. "He felt very confident. He talked—bragged maybe is more like it. His name is Jason LaRue and you were right, he did work for the government, the Treasury Department. Pa asked questions and so did I, and he told us the whole of it."

"Let me guess, he found the old file first," Canyon said.

"That's right. Then he came across the seven names in it, did some more searching, and as he told it, started to put together the basic facts. The half-million had been stolen and it had never been recovered. And the seven men whose names he had had quit their jobs and disappeared."

"So he deduced what most likely had happened over the years and was right about it," Canyon interjected.

"He took it from there and began to trace down each of the seven men as fast as he could. He said that the first thing he had to do was to make sure none of them talked to any of the others," Jennifer said.

"Killing them took care of that," Canyon said grimly. "Except for the last one, who he'd get to tell him where the money had been hidden."

"He told us how when he'd learned a government agent had been sent out on the case after the first four killings, he had to hire more men and speed up his searching. He said it wasn't that hard with most of the others who were working at one thing or another," Jennifer recounted.

"Only, when your pa heard about the first killing he got scared, a sixth sense maybe, and started running and hiding. So he became the last," Canyon said.

"And when I saw the other death notices, I got scared and started trying to trace him down," Jennifer said.

"And everyone tried to reach poor Alex Koosman. I was sitting on his tail to watch him and see if he knew anything more, you went to Pickett to meet him, and LaRue's killers did him in under our noses." Canyon grimaced.

"LaRue's a cold, merciless man, Canyon," Jennifer said.

"I'm sure of that." Canyon turned the palomino up onto a small spit of high land and pulled to a halt. "There's room for a few hours of sleep before morning. I'm going to take it. You'd best do the same."

"All right." Jennifer nodded and climbed down from the brown mare.

Canyon spread his bedroll out. "You're welcome to share it," he said. "It'll be more comfortable sleeping."

"There won't be anything else," she warned.

"Didn't expect there would be," he said. He shed his clothes, lay down on the bedroll, and Jennifer undressed in quick, swirling movements that pulled the loose nightgown over her with only the flash of bare skin. She lay down beside him but not touching.

She was silent beside him and he had just closed his eyes when she spoke, a small voice. "Thank you, Canyon O'Grady," she said.

"For what?" he asked.

"For my being here," she said. "I wish I didn't know it was all in the line of duty," she added, a mixture of tartness and sadness in her tone.

"Some of it was. Some of it wasn't. Take your pick," he said.

She lay still for another long moment and then rose on one elbow, half-turned, and her lips came to his with all the soft-sweet touch of her. "That's for the part that wasn't," she said when she pulled away, curled herself against him, and was asleep in moments.

He closed his eyes. Dawn would come all too quickly. He'd no idea what the day would bring except he was certain none of it would be good.

9

Canyon rose with the new day, peered down the small extension of high land, and grunted in satisfaction. He guessed he'd be able to see down to LaRue's camp, and it lay just below. He was dressed and watching on one knee as the camp woke, one man first, then another, and then the shout of surprise and alarm. Canyon watched the slightly portly figure leap to its feet. Jason LaRue ran to where Jennifer had been, halted, and quickly turned to scan the surrounding trees. The man's arms stretched stiffly at his sides, his fists clenched.

"You won't get him, O'Grady," Jason LaRue screamed. "You hear me, you bastard. You won't get him."

Canyon stayed motionless as Jennifer, wakened by the shout, came to his side. He saw her eyes find her father where he lay still tied.

LaRue walked over to Sam Shell, lifted the man to his feet, and smashed him across the face. Shell toppled to the ground. Jennifer's short cry half-froze in her throat. Canyon drew the ivory-gripped Colt, but LaRue had spun, barked orders to his men, and two of them seized Sam, guns jammed into his ribs. LaRue turned and surveyed the hills again.

"O'Grady," he shouted, "I know you're out there with the girl. I've two men holding guns on Sam Shell.

You shoot one, the other gets him. You shoot me, they both get him. That's the way it's going to be from now on. You make one move to get him and he's dead.''

Canyon stayed silent and watched LaRue's men gather their gear and begin to break camp. But two stayed with Sam Shell, guns pressed into his ribs. When they put him on his horse, they stayed alongside him, one on each side, guns trained on him. LaRue led the way on through the wooded terrain.

"What are we going to do?" Jennifer breathed, despair in her voice.

"Watch, wait, just as I told you, and maybe make a few moves on our own," Canyon said as he rose and swung onto the palomino.

"Such as?" Jennifer said as she quickly threw on clothes.

"I don't know yet," he answered. He waited for her to climb onto her horse, then led the way along the hill and watched the others ride below.

Jason LaRue stayed in the heavy tree cover, only glimpses of the riders visible when they passed a spot where the trees thinned for a few yards.

Canyon halted when the riders below reached such a spot, and his eyes narrowed as he peered down the hillside. "Get off your horse," he hissed sharply to Jennifer, who slid quickly to the ground, her brow furrowed.

"What is it? He's hiding from us down there," she said.

"That's only part of it," Canyon said. "Three of his men are missing. That means they're working their way up here to get us." Canyon dismounted, his eyes sweeping the hillside and halting at a spot a dozen yards higher where a series of rocky steps climbed atop one another, some only ledges a few feet apart. "That way," he said, and led Jennifer up to the stone steps. "You crawl in between the third and fourth," Canyon said. "There's just enough room for you to lay flat and scoot back in. You'll be out of sight there."

Jennifer nodded and he watched her climb, lie down flat, and squeeze herself between the oblong steps. She paused and called down to him. "How long do I stay here?"

"Until I come back for you," he said, and hurried back to where they'd left the horses, swung onto Cormac, and took the brown mare with him. He went into a gallop, reined up at a heavy thicket of white oak, and tethered the brown mare out of sight. He rode on alone, made a half-circle, and climbed upward until he halted against a stand of red cedar.

He swept the hillside below, from one side to the other, moving his eyes in a careful survey. He grunted as he picked up on a searcher to the far left, a second almost parallel to him but higher up on the hill. The third took longer to spot, but Canyon finally saw him, hanging back behind the first two. The first two were making the initial sweep, the third backing them up in case they missed anything.

Canyon watched the first two riders move carefully along the hillside, venturing in and out among the trees, searching for any sign of their quarry. Canyon swung from the great pale-bronze stallion and began to climb down the hillside on foot, staying low, ducking under branches so that no leaves moved to reveal his presence.

The two lead searchers had passed by and Canyon's eyes stayed on the third horseman as he scrambled down the hillside. He continued to duck, half-slide, half-run, and reached a clump of high brush as the third man drew near. Canyon dropped low, waited, watched the rider approach, the man's eyes scanning the ground above and below where he rode. He passed the brush where Canyon crouched, not more than six feet away. Canyon let him go on a half-yard before he bolted out of the brush and dove upward. The man half-spun in the saddle but Canyon's left arm was already curling around his neck, his leap carrying the man sideways from his horse. Canyon hit the ground atop the man, his right arm coming down with all his weight behind it onto the man's throat, and the only sound was the gagging, hoarse gasps as larynx and trachea were crushed.

Canyon pulled back, rose to one knee as the figure twitched, rolled, the wheezing gasps quickly growing hoarse until, with a final, rattling sound, they ceased altogether and the figure lay still. O'Grady got to his feet and quickly began to climb the hillside to where he'd left Cormack. When he retrieved the palomino, he rode farther so that he could see the other two riders ahead. He followed them until they halted and one half-rose in the saddle, waved an arm vigorously, and then both men turned and headed downhill.

Canyon's smile was grim as he waited till both men reached the bottom of the hill and crossed into the thick trees below to rejoin LaRue.

O'Grady turned the palomino around and rode back to the series of narrow stone ledges. The afternoon shadows were lengthening as he reached Jennifer, called softly, and she wriggled forward out of the narrow crawl space of rock.

"You hid away from them," she said as she pulled herself onto the mare.

"Did better than that," Canyon said. "Reduced the odds by one. LaRue will know what happened when his gunhand fails to join up with him."

"And he'll take it out on Pa," Jennifer said unhappily.

"Some, but not too much. He still wants his answers," Canyon told her. "Maybe tonight I can make him more nervous."

"You heard what he said, Canyon. They'll kill Pa if you try to get him."

"I'm not going to do that. I want to force LaRue into making a move—a mistake, I'm hoping. The only way to do that is to make him nervous." Canyon put the palomino into a gentle trot that led him downhill until he was in good view of the riders below, their tree cover thinning as darkness began to slide over the land.

Canyon saw the riders remained on each side of Sam Shell, their guns trained on the man. LaRue rode at the head of his band and plainly still waited for the third searcher to show. O'Grady grunted in satisfaction as he watched LaRue find a spot to camp near a small stream that ran down from the hills. Again, LaRue set up camp with his men spread out, two staying close to Shell.

Canyon watched Jason LaRue go to the edge of the camp and peer up into the darkened hills, plainly wondering why his man still hadn't returned.

"You'll have a long wait, my boy," Canyon murmured. He turned Cormack up along the hillside, and when he reached the stream that eventually coursed past LaRue's camp, he dismounted and brought some cold beef jerky from his saddlebag. "Let's eat and sleep a spell," he said to Jennifer, and he stretched out on the ground as soon as he finished the sparse meal. He slept and half-heard Jennifer restlessly toss and turn. She was sitting up, eyes wide, when he woke a few hours later.

"I couldn't sleep. I keep thinking about Pa and what's happening to him," she said.

Canyon thought for a moment and chose his words. It was not cruelty but kindness that governed his thoughts. She had to keep reality in hand or the hurt would be that much harder. "What's happening to your pa is his own fault," Canyon said. She snapped an angry look at him instantly but her lips tightened as she held back words. Canyon rose to his feet and looked at her. "I'll be leaving Cormac here with you," he said. "LaRue may have set out sentries and it'll be safer on foot."

"Canyon," she called out as he started to leave. "What happens if . . . if you don't come back?"

"Ride the palomino away from here," he said, and smiled. "And don't be of little faith." He hurried down the hillside in the night and left Jennifer, light-blue eyes wide with fear.

He moved under a three-quarter moon, hurried down the hillside, half-sliding in the steeper spots until he finally slowed when he reached the bottom. He dropped into a crouch and drew close to where LaRue had camped. He saw three figures standing, the others asleep, and he dropped to his stomach to crawl closer. The three men standing sentry gazed into the night in different directions, but they were inept excuses for a sentry. They peered nervously into the dark, squinting, trying to pry into the night when they should have been letting their other senses work for them.

Canyon moved still closer to the sleeping figures, creeping to the left of one of the sentries. He halted, surveyed the campsite, and saw Sam Shell on the other side, two men flanking each side even in sleep. Jason LaRue was also near his prisoner, Canyon was certain. He let his gaze slowly travel back over the other figures. He halted at one, nearest to where he was and apart from the others. He shifted his body and began to crawl forward again, silent as a diamondback on the prowl. It would have to be swift and silent, the kind of attack that always left him with a knot in his stomach. He'd never liked this kind of fighting and he always drew upon that wonderful weapon of the thinking man to be able to live with it. Rationalization, he muttered silently, the process that helps us justify the things we do in the name of justice. They were all killers, ruthless men who'd murder without a twinge of conscience. In fact, they had done just that, and LaRue, their dark-souled leader, was a man totally without mercy. It was rationalization, Canyon admitted, but it was also truth, and he paused only inches away from the sleeping figure.

When he moved again, the hunting knife was in his hand. He struck without raising his body, each move silent, delivered with deadly efficiency, and when he crawled backward, not even a blade of grass had rustled. When he'd had enough distance between the camp and himself, he rose and slowly, almost wearily, began to climb up the hillside.

Jennifer was awake when he reached the side of the stream, and her light-blue eyes greeted him with relief and questions. "No," he said as he slid himself to the ground. "No questions, no answers. It's not a happy night and it'll not be a happy dawn for LaRue. I'm going to sleep."

She came to him as he lay down and pressed herself against him in silence. He was glad for the comfort of her touch as he closed his eyes and plunged into the refuge of sleep, the tiny, bubbling sound of the stream a lullaby too pure for the night.

Canyon slept hard, determined to shut out the night, until the warmth of the morning sun woke him. He rose quickly, washed in the stream, and waited for Jennifer to be ready to ride. When she finished dressing, he led the way downhill and halted about halfway. LaRue's camp became clearly visible. He heard the swell of voices first, surprise at the grisly discovery, a murmur of uneasiness, and then LaRue stepped into the open again to sweep the hillside with his gaze. But the two men kept their guns on Sam, Canyon saw. LaRue extracted the kind of discipline he hadn't expected from his men, Canyon mused.

"You son of a bitch, O'Grady. I'll get you for this," Jason LaRue shouted into the hillside. "You won't get him, you hear me? You won't get him."

Canyon moved his horse from the tree line to where he could seen. "I'll get him, LaRue. And you, too," he called down. "If I have to do it one by one, I'll get all of you."

LaRue shouted curses below.

"Let's ride," Canyon barked, and sent Cormac into a trot.

Jennifer followed until he halted on the other side of the stream. "It seems to me you're only making him more determined to get his way with Pa," Jennifer said.

"He's down two men. He knows he can't stay in the tree cover forever. He'll have to come up with something. I'm hoping it'll be the wrong thing and I'll have him," Canyon said. He turned his eyes back down to the land at the bottom of the hills. LaRue had already broken camp and was riding hard now inside the tree cover. "Let's stay with him." Canyon urged the bronze stallion forward.

Below, LaRue continued to ride hard in the trees, but looking ahead from his position in the hills, Canyon saw the trees begin to thin out. He started to drop down lower in the hills and soon was only a few hundred yards above the bottom land. When the trees thinned to little more than clustered stands, LaRue sent his horses flat out. But the two men continued to flank Sam Shell, their guns fixed on Jennifer's father. Canyon could pick off Jason LaRue now with the big

Henry, but that would spell Sam's death. Again he fell back to following.

LaRue made a sudden turn and cut through a passage lined with low rocks. Canyon slowed, waited, and rode down to follow through the passage. He emerged at the other end to see a lake to one side and a long plateau with thick shrub grass from one side to the other. LaRue was a good few hundred yards ahead, and Canyon followed, Jennifer at his heels.

There was a low line of rocks at either side of the plateau where it ended in the distance. LaRue kept racing until he reached the left-hand wall of rocks. He halted, dismounted, and sent his men scurrying over the rocks, some disappearing into the sparse tree cover.

Canyon halted, unwilling to draw too close, but LaRue could see him and Jennifer where they had stopped, he knew.

"What's he doing?" Jennifer asked.

"Don't know. Can't figure it out yet," Canyon said, his frown focused on the scene at the end of the plateau. Suddenly two of LaRue's men returned with a thick branch. They cut off the limbs and put it into the ground between the two low lines of rock, hammered it deep with the end of their gun butts, and finally had themselves a stout stake. As he watched, while the two men kept their guns on Sam, others began to strip him down until he was a thin, bony figure they dragged to the stake.

Canyon heard Jennifer's gasp of anguished despair as they tied her father's naked form to the stake, binding him securely so he couldn't slide down. When they finished, half of the men hurried to the low rocks at one side and half to those on the other side.

Jason LaRue's voice echoed back to where Canyon watched at the end of the passage. "He's all yours,

O'Grady. All you have to do is come get him," the man said, and followed with a harsh laugh.

Canyon's eyes went to the sun that burned down on the treeless plateau, and he caught the anxiety in Jennifer's face. "That sun will burn him up damn quickly," he said, "but he'll be able to stand it for the rest of the day and the night will cool him down."

"What happens tomorrow?" she asked.

"We wait and see," Canyon said. He backed the palomino into the narrow passage just far enough so he could view the distant end of the plateau. "Relax, lass," he said to Jennifer as he dismounted. "There's nothing going to happen for now. LaRue understands that and knows I do."

"Relax?" she snapped. "How can I relax with my pa tied to a stake in the burning sun?"

"You can relax because there's nothing else you can do at this time," Canyon said, and lowered himself to the ground, leaned back against a rock, and gazed out across the plateau. "I don't know why, but this land hangs in the memory."

"You've been here before?" Jennifer asked.

"No, never, yet it has a familiar feel to it." Canyon frowned. "Strange!" He lapsed into silence.

The remainder of the day seemed never to end, the sun burning down hard on Sam Shell's naked form, but the twilight shadows finally came and the sun vanished. The nearly full moon rose and Canyon saw Jennifer's glance, the unsaid question hanging in it. "Forget it," he said more gruffly than he'd intended. "We'd no more make it to him by night than by day. They'd see us even if we crawled. It's all open land. That's why he picked it."

Canyon drew a deep sigh and decided not to give voice to the other certainty that hung in his mind, not this first night. He rose, took the bedroll from the palomino, and stretched it on the ground. He lay down on it and waited. It was a while before Jennifer stretched out beside him. She managed to sleep, finally, and he did the same until the morning came to the land and the sun woke him.

Jennifer woke as he did and followed his gaze across the plateau to the other end. LaRue and his men had put rain slickers and a tarpaulin up on poles made of branches to form cover for themselves.

Canyon silently swore as he saw Jennifer's eyes fixed on her father. He used his canteen to drink and wash as the sun quickly grew hot. The rocks of the narrow passage afforded shade for Jennifer and himself, but by midday the plateau was a sunburned stretch of land, Sam Shell quickly using up the last of his perspiration. He'd be dried out now, a parched, naked form that would soon turn red under the blazing rays. He heard Jason LaRue call to the man almost every hour, and though he couldn't catch the words, it really wasn't necessary. LaRue was offering the man only one thing: freedom for the answer to where the money had been hidden. But Sam still had consciousness enough to refuse.

LaRue was playing a dangerous game with Shell. The blazing sun could kill many a younger man with unexpected suddenness. But LaRue was counting on something else happening first, and he swore under his breath. He had underestimated the man's desperate cleverness, and Jennifer's words, bursting from her with an explosion of despair, gave voice to LaRue's tactics. "We have to do something," she said. "We can't just let him die before our eyes. Or maybe that doesn't matter to you."

"This is just what LaRue's banking on," Canyon said quietly. "He knows how to use people. He was going to get your pa to tell him where the money is by

146

working on you in front of him. That would have done it where direct torture wouldn't. Now he's using this to get to you to make me do something."

"Only he doesn't know that nothing gets to you," she flung at him, a sob in her voice, and he understood the bitterness that consumed her.

"I wouldn't say that."

"Then do something," Jennifer cried out with anguish and desperation.

"I'm not about to commit suicide, either, lass."

"So we just sit here and watch my pa die, that's what it comes back to, isn't it?"

Canyon looked away from her, his brow furrowed as he frowned out across the plateau. She wasn't all that far from wrong, he swore silently. He had no thoughts on how to reach Sam. There was no way to get to him without riding through the gauntlet of gunfire from LaRue's men. Yet he knew he had to do something, even if it were only a gesture for Jennifer. But what? He grimaced inwardly as the question hung in his mind without an answer. His thoughts were interrupted as LaRue stepped out from beneath the tarpaulin, cupped his hands around his mouth, and shouted across the plateau.

"You better come get him, O'Grady," he said. "He's not going to last much more than another day."

Canyon stepped out into the clear. "I'll be coming. You can count on that," he shouted back.

LaRue took another dozen steps closer. "I'll make a deal with you, O'Grady," he said. "Let the girl come and talk to him. She can get him to tell us where the money is. He'll listen to her. She gets him to talk and she can take him back with her. Everybody'll be happy."

Canyon smiled. "Everybody but me," he said. "No deal."

"Let the girl decide," LaRue said. "We'll be here waiting." The man turned and hurried back to the rocks and his tarpaulin cover.

Canyon returned to the passage to meet Jennifer's angry eyes.

"How could you turn him down?" she spit out. "He's right. Pa will listen to me and that's our only chance to save him. I'm going to take his deal."

"No," Canyon said. "That's no deal, only a lot of empty promises. Soon as your pa tells him what he wants to know, he's dead for sure. Nothing's changed. Except you'll be dead along with him."

"Maybe you're wrong. I think all he wants is to find out where the money is and run. He said to let me decide. I've decided. I'm going out to Pa."

"He's smart, the way a weasel is smart. He's working on you. He expects you'll do exactly what you're doing."

"It's past time for your suspicions," Jennifer snapped, whirled, and started toward her horse. "I'm going to Pa. I'm going to give LaRue what he wants and bring Pa back."

Canyon reached out and caught her arm and spun her back. "No," he said sharply. "There is no deal, dammit. He can't afford to just let you ride off with your pa. He's a cold, clever killer. You just don't want to see it. Or maybe you can't see it any longer. I'm not letting you go."

She pulled away from him and stared at him with frustration, pain, and anguish in her eyes. "You'd stop me from trying to save Pa's life?" she accused.

"No, I'll stop you from getting yourself killed along with him," Canyon said.

"Then give me something better," Jennifer demanded. "You have nothing better and that's the truth." Canyon half-shrugged, the gesture an admission. "You've nothing to offer, but you won't let me take the only chance we have. Did you ever think that maybe you're too consumed with distrust and hate? Did you ever think that maybe you can't see straight or think straight about this any longer?"

Canyon let a sharp, harsh half-laugh escape his lips. "No," he answered.

"Well, maybe you should think about it," she said.

"A man that doubts himself is lost," Canyon told her. "And I know Jason LaRue's breed." He drew a deep sigh and met Jennifer's angry eyes again. "Give me through the night," he said. "Give me a little more time to come up with something."

She frowned, turned away, and refused to look at him as she let the two words drop from her lips. "All right." She strode to the edge of the passage and sat down against a rock to stare across the plateau at the distant, naked figure on the stake.

Canyon swore silently at himself and at Jason LaRue as he sat down near Jennifer. He had bought time, more in hope that something might happen to change the standoff than to find a way to rescue Sam. He had racked his brains on that and come up with nothing, and he continued to search his mind for some plan that had even a faint chance of succeeding.

The sun was burning down into the midafternoon when Canyon saw LaRue and two of his men leave their cover and go to Shell. He managed to see that LaRue had a canteen with him as they halted at the stake.

"They're going to give Pa some water," Jennifer said, gratitude flooding her voice. "Dammit, Canyon, he's trying to keep him alive so we'll take his deal."

"Look again," Canyon bit out as he watched LaRue pass the canteen back and forth under Sam's mouth. LaRue whispered to the old man, waved the canteen again, and then hurried back to the shade cover with his two gunhands. "He didn't give him a drop. He was using the water to get him to open up," Canyon said, and listened to Jennifer's sob of despair. He leaned his head back and watched the burning sun make its way across the sky. The day was nearing an end when LaRue came out from his shade again. Canyon rose and stepped a half-dozen yards into the open.

"The deal holds till morning, O'Grady," LaRue shouted. "Another morning of sun and it'll be too late for the old man."

"You lose, too," Canyon said.

"Oh, no, we're watching him real careful. He'll give it to us. He's near breaking now. But it'll be too late for you and the girl to save him then," the man said.

Canyon saw Jennifer's accusing eyes turn to him. "You gave me till morning," he reminded her.

She put her hands to her face as if to hide from the world.

Canyon turned to the distant figure again. "I'll be coming to get him tonight," he called. "The old man first and then you." It was an empty threat, of course, but it would let LaRue think he was going to win it all. He'd wait with a mixture of concern and confidence and spend the night in sleepless waiting.

Canyon grunted bitterly, glad for even the most minor triumph. He returned to the mouth of the passageway and watched the sun slip down over the horizon. Twilight came to embrace the plateau and Canyon's brow furrowed.

"It's just come to me," he said, and Jennifer looked up. "Why this place has a familiar feel to it. I remember now, in the dusk. It's very much like the great moors in Donegal, wide and flat with the mists of the marshes curling around it in the dusk."

"Damn you," Jennifer exploded. "My pa's being

baked to death and you're talking about geography and old memories. I hate you, Canyon O'Grady.'' She spun, flung herself down with her face to the rocks, and he listened to her angry, despairing sobs. She had exploded with all the pent-up frustrations inside her. Suddenly he felt the furrow slide across his brow. Other things could explode. He felt the excitement surge through him. It was a chance, perhaps a suicidal chance, yet maybe the only one.

He leapt to his feet, ran to his saddlebag, and brought out the sticks of dynamite he had nestled there. Jennifer had turned at his sudden movement and stared at him as he held the dynamite aloft in his hand. ''The Lord writes straight in crooked ways,'' he said. He took his lariat from the horse and folded himself against the rocks. ''LaRue is expecting me to come get your pa tonight. I wouldn't think of disappointing him.''

''Don't talk in circles,'' Jennifer admonished.

''I'm going in,'' Canyon said. ''With the dynamite.''

He rose, went to the saddle, and brought out almost the last of the beef jerky. ''Eat some now. I have to wait for the moon to come up and give me light.''

Jennifer took two of the sticks of food and chewed slowly as Canyon sat back and watched the moon rise to cast its pale light. It had grown full and it gave enough light for what he had to do.

He cut a length of the lariat and began to unravel the rope into slender strands. Carefully, he tied one end of the strands to the fuses already in place on the sticks of dynamite. Then he laid a long piece of the strands on the ground, put a match to one end, and began to count as it slowly burned. When he'd counted off two minutes, he cut the strands and snuffed out the flame. ''Now all I have to do is measure the burned part," he murmured as Jennifer looked on. He took a length of fresh strand, laid it against the charred line on the ground, and cut it the same length.

"What makes you think they'll let you get close enough?" Jennifer asked.

"Two things," he answered. "They'll want me right in their cross fire before they start shooting. They won't want to risk missing me. And second, I'll be giving them a little something to occupy their attention, keep them off balance."

Jennifer's eyes were grave. "It could go wrong."

"It could," he admitted. "But it's the only chance. There is no tomorrow, lass, just as there is no deal. Now I'm going to get some shut-eye for a spell. I don't like arriving at a party too early." He lay down, stretched out, and Jennifer came to lay alongside him. She stayed against him, warm and soft, until he woke with the moon high in the sky, the plateau covered with its pale silver light, a wispy cover of mist hugging the ground. He rose and went to the pale-bronze horse; Jennifer went with him and her arms encircled his neck.

"Can you ever forgive all the rotten things I said?"

"There's nothing to forgive. They didn't come from the heart. They came from the dark fears inside you." He smiled.

Her lips pressed hard against his until she finally drew back.

"Now that's much better," he said. "You stay here. I'll call for you."

"I'll be listening, you know that," she said, and he nodded as he rode from the mouth of the passageway, a lone rider moving out across the ground-covering mists, the palomino glistening under the full moon. He walked Cormac slowly and knew they'd not pick him out till he was halfway across the plateau.

When he reached that point, he heard the sudden

shouts from ahead and he smiled as he lifted his voice, the rich sound of it carrying clearly to the end of the plateau. They would hear it, of course, look at one another, frown, unable to believe their ears. They'd watch and listen and be distracted without realizing it. Jason LaRue in particular, he was certain. LaRue was not a man who could understand a grand gesture. He was not a man who could comprehend anything but his cold, killing ways. He would stare and wonder and be fascinated, and that would be enough. Canyon lifted his voice again, more strongly now.

"It's of a brave young highwayman,
    his story we will tell.
His name was Willie Brennan
    and in Ireland he did dwell,
'twas on the Gilworth mountains,
    he commenced his wild career,
and many a wealthy nobleman before him
    shook with fear.

"Oh, it's Brennan on the moor,
    Brennan on the moor,
Oh, brave and undaunted,
    was young Brennan on the moor.

"One day upon the highway,
    young Willie he went down.
He met the Mayor of Cashel,
    a mile outside the town.
The mayor he knew his features
    and he said, 'young man,' he said,
'your name is Willie Brennan and
    you'll come along with me.'

"Oh, it's Brennan on the moor,
    Brennan on the moor,

Oh, brave and undaunted was
    young Brennan on the moor. . . ."

Canyon continued to sing as he reached the facing rows of rocks. He could almost hear Jason LaRue growling to his men. "What the hell is he doing?" LaRue would be asking, consternation still gripping his narrow-eyed face. Canyon put a match to the two fuses and muttered a silent prayer. If he'd made an error in timing, he and young Willie Brennan would be all over the moor, he told himself grimly.

The fuses burned, a small hissing sound, and he was almost abreast of the two rows of rocks now. They'd be lifting their guns to fire, still frowning as he continued to sing at the top of his voice. Moving his arms as little as possible, he flung the two sticks of dynamite as the fuses were almost at an end.

He threw one to his left with is right hand and the other to his right with his left hand. The moment the dynamite sticks left his hands he flattened himself atop Cormac's back and sent the palomino into a gallop as the first volley of shots rang out. He heard them whistle by only inches over his back. Obviously, LaRue and the others hadn't seen the two sticks sailing through the air yet, but suddenly Canyon heard the shout of panic as they saw the dynamite. The shots were drowned by the shattering explosions that rent the night air just over the two rows of rocks.

Though he had almost reached the stake, Canyon felt the air whipping at him and the horse and he reined to a halt as he leapt to the ground, fell, and rolled over to land only a few feet from Sam Shell's naked body.

Behind him, the sound of the explosions died away and he heard a few scattered moans, a sharp, guttural cough that ended as soon as it began, and then all was silence. Canyon took his canteen from his saddlebag and went to the naked, half-shriveled figure, lifted the spout to Sam's lips, and the man drank with eager, gasped sounds. Canyon gave him just enough to take away the worst of the parched thirst and then cut the ropes binding the thin body to the stake. He caught Sam as the man sank to the ground, and gave him more water to drink.

Shell finally opened his parched, sunburned eyelids to stare at the big flame-haired man in front of him.

"You'll be all right now," Canyon said. He was about to tell Sam to stay there and drew the words back. Shell wasn't strong enough to go anywhere. Canyon rose, drew the big Colt, and moved toward the line of rocks at his left. He stepped behind them, gun ready to fire as he took in the bodies that lay there, some partly blown apart, others intact but just as dead from the force of the explosion that had ripped the air over their heads. He went to the other row and saw much the same scene, more arms and legs torn away there.

He holstered the gun and turned to the far end of the plateau. "Jennifer, come on, lass." He waited till he glimpsed the horse racing across the ground, then he returned to where Sam lay against the stake. He managed to draw trousers and shirt over the man's reddened body. "You'll need the protection when the morning sun comes," he said, and Sam managed to nod.

Jennifer rode to a skidding halt and jumped down from the horse, and Canyon stepped away as she cradled her father in her arms. He let her have time enough with the old man and then stepped forward again. "Let's get away from here," he said.

"Yes." Jennifer nodded. "I'll hold him in the saddle with me. You can tie his horse behind."

"Good enough," Canyon said.

They set a slow pace from the plateau, found the land beyond at the bottom of a slope where a good cover of hackberry appeared. He halted, helped Sam from the saddle, and put the old man on a bed of soft nut moss under a thick-branched tree. "We'll let him sleep the day in the shade," he told Jennifer. "Might do just the same myself."

She nodded, and when he had everyone settled down, he lowered himself to the ground and welcomed the relief of sleep.

When morning came, he woke and saw Jennifer giving her father a long sip from her canteen. When she finished, she lay down beside him and returned to sleep. Most of the day passed that way, Jennifer waking regularly to administer water to her father while the shade protected him from the sun.

It was late afternoon when Canyon rose to his feet and was surprised to see Sam's eyes clear, only his burned face any indication of what he'd been through. He was a tough old bird, Canyon conceded. "I figured we'd ride in the cool of the night," he said.

Shell pulled himself to his feet. "Good enough. I'll ride my own horse," he said.

"Are you sure you're up to it, Pa?" Jennifer asked.

"I am," he answered with a touch of pride.

Jennifer turned to Canyon. "Nothing that's happened makes any difference, does it?" she said, resignation in her voice. "You're still going to take him in."

"I am," Canyon said. "But I've been thinking." He turned to Sam. "If you brought the money back with you, or most of it, it'd help. It might make the difference between a noose and a little time in jail. Or they might, taking your age, decide restitution was

156

enough." He paused, let the words sink in. "Where's the money hidden, Sam?"

"Not far from here, a day's ride maybe," the man said.

"Let's get it," Canyon said.

Shell nodded and it seemed a wave of relief passed through his lined face. "Yes, let's get it," he agreed.

Canyon swung onto the palomino as the night began to descend, and he let Sam lead the way, the pace haltingly slow.

"Do you really think the money will help?" Jennifer asked Canyon as she rode beside him.

"Very much," he told her, and she gave a little sigh of relief.

They rode for most of the night, and when Sam was too tired to go on, they bedded down under thick shade trees again. Canyon slept hard through the morning and woke with the midafternoon sun moving across the sky. He frowned as he rose. An uneasiness had come upon him and he didn't know why. Perhaps it was all going too well too suddenly, he told himself. He woke the others.

They rode at a slow pace again as night came, halted in the small morning hours, and it was near dawn when he heard Sam wake and sit up. "Let's go on. I'm well enough and it's only a few hours away," the man said.

"Fine with me," Canyon agreed. But as he climbed onto the palomino, he frowned again. The uneasiness still stayed with him, but he swung into line behind Sam Shell. The man led the way down between two hills, climbed a third, and the dawn broke as they emerged at a place where a wide, rushing river of water cascaded down from between two more hills. Shell stopped and Canyon halted next to him, his eyes on the man's face. He saw Sam stare at the rushing waters, his jaw drop open.

"This was the place," he murmured. "A small ravine between these hills."

"You sure you're not making a mistake, Pa?" Jennifer asked.

Shell slid from his horse. "No mistake. That ridge of alders up there, running all along the top, that was the mark. But it was a dry ravine," he said, and continued to stare at the racing waters.

"It was long ago. The land changes. Storms make changes," Canyon said. "This has become a high land river, probably diverted here by a mud slide God knows how long ago."

"And the money?" Jennifer asked.

"Washed away with the rest of the land that was here," Canyon said. "Washed away in mud and silt as the waters carved a new bed for themselves."

"Oh, God, oh, my God," Sam breathed. "All of it for nothing. All of it wasted."

"O'Grady!"

The single word rent the air and Canyon didn't wait to see where it came from as he dived headlong, hit the ground, and rolled. The shot exploded as he dived and he heard Jennifer's scream. He came up on one knee, his eyes focused on the higher land, and he saw the portly figure, rifle to its shoulder. Jason LaRue fired again and Canyon dived sideways as the bullet tore through the top of his shoulder, ripping a hole in his shirt. But he had the Colt in hand and he fired as LaRue spun and ducked into the trees. The shot missed.

Canyon leapt up, ran to the palomino, and vaulted into the saddle. He sent the horse racing upward at a full gallop. He could hear LaRue's horse crashing through brush. Canyon raced to his right, then upward again, Cormack taking the uneven ground without breaking stride.

LaRue came into sight. The man heard his approach, whirled his horse around, and brought the rifle up to fire again. Canyon dropped low in the saddle and the shot went over his head as he fired the Colt, three shots that echoed in the woods.

LaRue started to turn his horse again, and then, as if it were an afterthought, he toppled sideways out of the saddle to lay still on the ground. Only when Canyon spurred the palomino closer did he see that LaRue's one leg, from the knee down, had been swathed in makeshift bandages, caked with dried blood.

Canyon drew a deep sigh as he holstered the Colt and rode back to the water to see Jennifer on the ground, Sam in her arms. Her tear-filled eyes turned to him as he dismounted. "That first bullet hit him," she said.

Canyon reached down, lifted her, refused her attempts to continue to cling to the man, and took her to the side.

Her eyes went to him, pain and anger in their light-blue depths. "You don't have to take him in now," she said bitterly.

"That's right," he said. "It's over. Case closed."

She looked away, eyes on the ground. "We have to bury him someplace."

"Right here," Canyon said. He didn't need to spell out more for her, and she nodded slowly and sank to the ground. He used a small spade he had in his saddlebag and was grateful for the softness of the earth near the rushing waters.

"My fault, this last part," he said as he dug. "I should've looked more closely back at the plateau. They just all looked dead. Obviously, LaRue wasn't. He bandaged himself, got a horse that was still alive, and followed us. We went slow, but that was fine with him, I'm sure. I should have looked harder."

He finished digging and made a crude wooden cross.

Jennifer came to him. "None of it was your fault, Canyon O'Grady," she said. "Just take me with you. Make me forget. Let your arms become my world for a while."

Canyon held her. It seemed a good idea. Perhaps the only good thing to come out of all of it. It had been a tangled web of greed and deceit that had woven down through the long years. Perhaps Meriwether Lewis had been the only good man who had died because of it. The others were all tainted in one way or another. Shakespeare had it right: "The evil that men do lives after them," Canyon mused aloud. "And lives and lives and sometimes finally swallows them up in it," he added.

He swung Jennifer onto the saddle with him and felt her warm softness against him. The flesh was as good a place as any to forget the spirit. It was always itself, without lies and deceits.

"Let's go, lass. We've a lot of forgetting to do," he said as he sent the pale-bronze horse into the shadows of the afternoon sun.

KEEP A LOOKOUT!

The following is the opening section from the third novel in the action-packed new Signet Western series CANYON O'GRADY.

CANYON O'GRADY #3
MACHINE GUN MADNESS

Short Creek, Missouri, 80 miles south of Kansas City near the Kansas border, July 14, 1860. The trek to find Hirum Merchant and his amazing new gun that fired 600 rounds a minute!

Ten Osage warriors had been circling the small frame house and yi-yipping just out of pistol range for a half hour. All of the warriors were mounted on war ponies, all had bows and arrows, and one carried an old flintlock rifle he might not know how to fire. They darted in toward the door yelling and screaming, then slanted away, guiding their horses with only their knees.

Now, one raced forward on his war pony and sent an arrow smashing through the kitchen window.

Soon all of them shot arrows into the windows of the small house. One of the braves paused at the side to blow a coal into a flame, then lit a torch and raced toward the house.

Jolting through the yells and calls of the Osage came the snarling report of a heavy rifle. A warrior with a burning torch and a row of eagle feathers on his brow-band slammed off his war pony with a .52-caliber chunk of lead through his heart and lodged near his backbone. He sprawled in the Missouri dust never to move again.

Before the Indians realized they were under attack, a second report sounded and another Osage took a bullet high in the shoulder, sending him half off his pony. The warrior clung to the horse's mane slumping forward as he raced off toward a creek a quarter of a mile away.

In a clump of brush two-hundred yards from the house, a man lay, his eye pressed to the sight of a Henry rifle. He tracked another Osage, led him a foot and fired. The attacking Indian took the round in his chest, screamed, and fell off his war pony.

Now the Indians looked in his direction, attracted by the pall of blue smoke the three shots had left just at the edge of the brush.

Four of the Osage turned and screeched at each other, then charged his position. The big man with a shock of flame-red hair who lay in the brush rolled toward a big cottonwood tree trunk and came to a kneeling position. He worked the trigger guard of the Henry quickly, blasting lead at the charging Indians.

He knocked two of them off their horses before they were within fifty yards of him. They wheeled and headed back as he fired the last of the eight shots from the Henry. He had drawn his big ivory-gripped Colt revolver, but when he saw them wheel away, he up-ended the Henry and quickly pulled out the empty tube from the butt of the weapon and pushed in a new tube filled with seven new .52-caliber rounds.

He chambered one and then sent six more shots at

the Osage who now streaked away using the small house as cover against his rifle fire. When he was sure they were gone, the tall man rose up and walked cautiously into the open where he bent and checked the first of the fallen Indians. Two were dead. He had just bent over the third when a woman's voice cried out a warning.

He swung around, the Colt coming with him, and he fired automatically at one of the wounded Indians who was finding the strength to throw a knife at him. The .44 slug took the Osage in the left eye and drove him back into the dirt.

Canyon O'Grady checked the last two bodies, determined that they were well dead, and looked up at the girl standing in the back door of the small house. First he saw the blue dress, nipped in the waist, flaring at the breasts, and buttoned protectively to wrist and chin.

Then he saw a billowing mass of long blonde hair cascading around her shoulders. The six-gun she held seemed out of place and he noted that wisps of gunsmoke still came from the muzzle.

Her pale green eyes looked up at him as he walked forward. She saw a strapping man well over six feet, a shock of red hair, and crackling blue eyes in a roguish face.

She seemed to beat back tears as she smiled. "You saved my life. I thank you."

"Aye, lass. Osage, I'd say," he said.

There was a lilt of Ireland in his voice.

"Yes, they come through here now and then. Usually a shot or two near them and they move on."

"These were unusual then."

She held the six-gun in front of her, not pointing it at him, but ready to.

"You just passing by?" she asked.

"Might be. Looking for Hirum Merchant. In town they told me he lived here."

"Sometimes. He's gone right now. What would you want with him?"

"Business. Hear tell he's a gunsmith."

The girl nodded, her eyes a bit wary, blonde hair rustling. Now he saw that her nose was finely made, her eyebrows were soft and blonde, and her mouth was set now in a firm pink line. A dimple would dent one cheek if she smiled, he was sure.

"Yes, Pa's an excellent gunsmith, but he doesn't hire out right now."

"Still and all, I need to see him."

"Likes of you is why he left two months ago. So many people came to see him he couldn't get his work done."

"That work he's doing is why I need to see him. I'd say I did you a favor, lass, with those Osage. Where I come from people are proud to repay favors. I think it's time for you to return the favor to me. Them Osage were about to burn you right out of that house. I'd imagine you know what they'd do to the likes of a beautiful girl like you once you were out of rounds for that revolver of yours."

"I know what they would do." She sighed and lifted her glance to lock with his. The revolver swung down and she pointed it at the ground. "I'm truly grateful for your help. I was so frightened I could hardly shoot. First I liked it out here away from the rest of town, but today I didn't."

"I still need to find your father," he pressed.

Excerpt from *MACHINE GUN MADNESS*

He could see the emotions sweeping through her: gratitude to him, loyalty to her father. At last she sighed once more. "You come inside and I'll sit you down to some coffee and we'll talk some."

The house was neat, no dirty dishes on the ledge at the side of the kitchen. She took out a clean coffee pot and made a quick, fast-burning fire in a small cast iron stove.

"Coffee be ready soon. I still can't tell you where Pa went. He made me promise. Said it was important that he get done with his work."

Canyon sat down in the offered chair and watched the sleek young woman getting the coffee started. When she turned, the movement brought the swell of her full breasts tight against the gingham dress. He watched in open admiration.

"The importance of your Pa's work is why I'm here, Miss Merchant. My name is Canyon O'Grady, and I want to help your father get his work done."

"If you're looking to buy it, he isn't ready to sell."

"I don't want to buy it, lass."

"At least I know you're full of Irish blarney. I'm sorry, I can't help you."

Canyon looked out the window. "Time was when a person would be grateful for even the smallest favor. Now someone gets her life saved and it's good for only a fine thank you and a beautiful smile."

"Pa said he was working on something important."

"That he is. The United States Army and the President of the United States are both highly interested in Hirum Merchant's new rapid firing gun. We know a little about it. We have also heard that others are trying to steal it from him."

"The President of the United States?" She looked

up at him with awe, then suspicion. ''The President? I really don't know whether to believe that or not.''

''You should. You probably haven't heard that there are a lot of people right now interested in making a gun like your father is working on. There are men from our own country who have said that they will find your father, steal his gun and then begin to manufacture them. These men are well known for their crooked dealings and will stop at nothing to get what they want. The president sent me to find your father and protect him.''

The girl sat down slowly. ''You really mean it, don't you?'' Her eyes went wide and she held out her hand. ''Pleased to meet you, Canyon O'Grady. I'm Elizabeth Merchant.'' She continued to stare at him.

''You actually talked to President Buchanan?''

''Yes, six or seven times. I work for him. That's why I'm here. We think your father needs some protection. We have information that at least one foreign nation as well as this band of Americans are out to get your father's invention away from him by any means possible.''

''Oh, they can't do that! Pa has worked on this new gun for over two years now. We've almost starved at times. Then he'd have to take work as a gunsmith at some town. But every night—'' Elizabeth stopped. ''Oh, dear. I wonder if he's safe where he went? He didn't know somebody might actually try to steal the gun.''

''Someone could do far worse than that to your father, Miss Merchant.''

The pretty young woman frowned for a moment, then stood and paced up and down in the small kitchen.

She looked at Canyon two or three times and finally stopped.

"Say Pa is in danger, and there are these men trying to find and hurt him. How do I know that you're not just another one of them?"

"You have only my word on that, Miss Merchant. And my open, honest, Irish face."

"You don't have any kind of badge or a paper, or anything? Even a U.S. Marshall has papers."

He took a folded paper from his wallet. It was signed by President Buchanan and said Canyon O'Grady was a United States Agent. Everyone was urged to give him complete cooperation.

She read the paper and gave it back to him, then went to the cupboard and took out a dish of ham and beans and put it in a pot she placed on the iron stove. Then she added two sticks to the fire. She poured the coffee and watched Canyon.

"I'm not sure I trust you, Canyon O'Grady. Irishmen are not my favorite people."

Canyon grinned broadly. "You're sounding a little Irish yourself. Samuel Johnson said: 'The Irish are a fair people, they never speak well of one another.' But then you know that Sam Johnson was an Englishman, so what can you expect."

"Not saying I will, but if I was to be convinced I should take you to my Pa, would you let me keep my six-gun?"

"Yes, I would. Two of them and a derringer and a knife if you want to carry them. But you don't have to take me anywhere. You can stay right here. Just tell me where he went so I can get to him as quickly as possible."

"No, I won't tell you a thing. If I decide to, I'll

take you there and watch you closely. There's too much blarney in you for my way of thinking.'' She stared at him a minute, then shrugged. ''Near sundown now. If you split me some wood, I can finish warming us some supper. Tomorrow morning I'll decide what I'm going to do.''

''Where's the woodpile?''

A half hour later he came in with an armload of wood and stacked it neatly in the woodbox. The supper was simple but adequate, and the coffee was hot.

When the dishes were put away she pointed at the door. ''Canyon O'Grady, take your Irish wit and your bedroll and find a spot to sleep in the woods. I'm inside with the door bolted and broken windows covered—and my six-gun under my pillow. I'll decide tomorrow.''

''Alright,'' Canyon agreed. ''But I'll be ready to go tomorrow. I know you'll want the two of us to find your Pa and warn him about the danger he's in.''

He watched her a moment, and saw her working on the big problem. Then he said good night, went out the door, and waited until he heard the bolt slam home. Canyon found a spot in the brush where he had fired at the Indians. He wanted to give the redskins plenty of room to return and pick up their dead as soon as it was dark. He was surprised they hadn't done so already. They would float in during darkness, like ghost dancers, retrieving their slain friends and would be no threat. The Osage, like most Indians, do not like to fight at night.

Canyon stretched out on his bedroll. The girl was worried about her father. He figured that she would decide come morning to go find him and would take

Canyon along. There was really no other decision she could make.

Before he fell to sleep, Canyon went over his assignment again as he had been briefed by Major General Silas Warrenton. Many times President Buchanan himself gave Canyon his orders, but this problem was too urgent and there was no time for Canyon to go to Washington.

Canyon had been in St. Louis finishing up a case and had kept General Warrenton informed. He received a telegram a few days ago telling him to remain in place, a courier would be coming to hand-deliver a first class secret document.

The courier met Canyon at his hotel, the Mid Western, had him write his name on a card, and compared it with a sample he brought with him. Then the courier took out a photograph and studied it against the real thing. When he was convinced that Canyon was who he said he was, he had him sign off on a receipt for the goods and went down to catch the next train back to Washington.

Canyon went up to his third-floor room and unsealed the envelope and began to read.

"To: Canyon O'Grady, United States Agent.

"From: Silas Warrenton, Major General USA., Military Aide to President Buchanan.

"At once proceed to Kansas City, Missouri, and then south to a small town called Short Creek, and contact a gunsmith named Hirum Merchant.

"Our information is that he is in the final stages of development of a new kind of rapid firing gun that, if successful, will be a major leap forward in weaponry.

"The United States Government is interested in protecting Mr. Merchant from any outside influence, and to be sure that he has both the time and facilities to finish work on his weapon.

"When you contact Mr. Merchant explain to him the President's concern, and urge him to be the guest of the government at the nearest United States military post or fort where he will be given space and equipment and board and room as he works on his project.

"Problems: We are not sure that Mr. Merchant is at the above given town. He may have left. He has a daughter who may or may not be with him. Your first job is to find the man. Your second task is to protect him from all those who would try to buy, steal, or destroy his new weapon, and to safeguard Merchant himself.

"Second problem is that there is at least one foreign power now in Missouri with several agents, who is determined to capture Mr. Merchant and steal his ideas, his prototype and plans and perhaps kidnap Mr. Merchant himself and take them out of the country.

"While preparing this briefing, I discover that there is now a second foreign power with several men in Missouri with the sole purpose of finding Mr. Merchant and evaluating his weapon. If they like it they will attempt to buy it. If he won't sell, then they will simply steal it, probably kill Hirum Merchant and return with the gun to their own nation. You must prevent this at all costs.

"With the growing concern for finding new military weapons, our President feels that we must meet both of these threats by protecting Mr. Merchant.

"You may requisition troops and weapons from any fort or army installation, including Fort Leavenworth just outside of Kansas City, Kansas. I have this day sent the fort commander a telegram authorizing such assistance from Fort Leavenworth.

"Wire your receipt of these orders at once and wire me at any time you have need of assistance or direction and upon completion of the assignment."

There was the scrawled signature of General Warrenton at the bottom of the third sheet.

Canyon had sent a quick wire to Washington, put his magnificent palomino mount in a livery stable, and caught a night train to Kansas City. There was no way he could send his mount by train to Kansas City on such short notice. He bought a horse for the two-day ride to Short Creek, which had no stage service.

Now laying in the brush up from the house, Canyon heard something. He looked back at the house. A figure ran silently toward the building, then went around it and soon found one of the Indian bodies. The warrior picked up the corpse, looked around, and then hurried into the darkness.

Canyon saw two other Osage retrieving their dead, then the stillness was complete again. He waited for a half hour, and when the Indians didn't return, he closed his eyes and went to sleep. If anything moved within fifty feet of him he would be awake instantly with his big Army revolver in his fist.

Morning came suddenly on the plains with the sun bursting over the flat land horizon a hundred miles away, or so it seemed. Canyon was up, and had slipped into his boots and gunbelt, then shaved with cold water from his canteen. He sliced the whiskers off with a straight razor by feel. One of these days he was going to get a small metal mirror to carry with him.

He heard the house door open. Elizabeth came out,

looked around, and went to the outhouse. She carried the revolver. He thought it was a .32 caliber. Big enough to make a nasty hole. Canyon packed up his gear and tied it on his saddle, tightened up the cinch, and led the big bay mare down to the edge of the creek where she drank her fill. He ground-tied her in some fresh grass and walked back to the house.

Elizabeth had just arrived at the door when he got there.

"Morning," he said.

She stared up at him and she looked as if she hadn't slept too well. "All right, all right, I've decided to lead you to where my Pa is supposed to be. If all this is true you've been telling me, he might have left that spot as well, but we'll go and try to find him."

"Good, I was hoping you would say that."

"I've traveled before. I have a sack of food ready. Some bacon, eggs in a jar, two loaves of bread I baked yesterday, and some tins and dried goods. Couple of pots and a frying pan. You might find us a rabbit along the way. Breakfast first, flapjacks while we still have milk, and syrup."

They left a half hour later. She closed the door, locked it, and put the key on top of the door frame. Then she turned and frowned at him, her pretty face tense.

"Just so we get this straight. You are coming with me, not the other way around. I know where we're going. I also have my thirty-two caliber six-gun and I know how to use it. Right now I don't have any good reason to distrust you, and I hope it stays that way."

She watched him a moment. "Any comments?"

"Only that you don't have to frown so much, it ruins your beautiful smile."

"Blarney will get you nowhere with me, Mr. O'Grady. Now let's ride."

They turned south and a little west. Canyon had admired the sleek way she fit into the ladies riding trousers that she had on. They outlined her round little bottom delightfully. She wore a brown blouse and a light jacket and a straw hat with a wide brim with a tie under her chin.

She set a good pace down a country road, across a field, and toward the early morning smokes of a village five miles away. They had just passed through a grove of trees when Canyon called sharply.

"Elizabeth! We've got company. Back to those trees, right now!"

She saw the five men racing toward them across the field from the direction they had come. They were still three hundred yards away but coming at a gallop.

Canyon checked to see that the Henry carbine was still in his saddle boot, then kicked the bay in the flanks, and surged into the brushline. He tied his mount, grabbed the Henry, and ran to the edge of the brush.

Only two of them came straight on. The other three had circled around to the side.

"Damn!" Canyon spat. Whoever it was planned on making a fight of it. So be it, Canyon growled to himself and lifted the Henry and sent a round over the heads of the two onrushing men who were waving revolvers in the air. He'd find out quickly how serious they were about a fight.

Ⓢ SIGNET WESTERNS BY JON SHARPE

(0451)

RIDE THE WILD TRAIL

☐ THE TRAILSMAN #62: HORSETHIEF CROSSING (147146—$2.75)

☐ THE TRAILSMAN #63: STAGECOACH TO HELL (147510—$2.75)

☐ THE TRAILSMAN #64: FARGO'S WOMAN (147855—$2.75)

☐ THE TRAILSMAN #66: TREACHERY PASS (148622—$2.75)

☐ THE TRAILSMAN #67: MANITOBA MARAUDERS (148908—$2.75)

☐ THE TRAILSMAN #68: TRAPPER RAMPAGE (149319—$2.75)

☐ THE TRAILSMAN #69: CONFEDERATE CHALLENGE (149645—$2.75)

☐ THE TRAILSMAN #70: HOSTAGE ARROWS (150120—$2.75)

☐ THE TRAILSMAN #71: RENEGADE REBELLION (150511—$2.75)

☐ THE TRAILSMAN #72: CALICO KILL (151070—$2.75)

☐ THE TRAILSMAN #73: SANTA FE SLAUGHTER (151399—$2.75)

☐ THE TRAILSMAN #74: WHITE HELL (151933—$2.75)

☐ THE TRAILSMAN #75: COLORADO ROBBER (152263—$2.75)

☐ THE TRAILSMAN #76: WILDCAT WAGON (152948—$2.75)

☐ THE TRAILSMAN #77: DEVIL'S DEN (153219—$2.75)

☐ THE TRAILSMAN #78: MINNESOTA MASSACRE (153677—$2.75)

☐ THE TRAILSMAN #79: SMOKY HELL TRAIL (154045—$2.75)

☐ THE TRAILSMAN #80: BLOOD PASS (154827—$2.95)

☐ THE TRAILSMAN #82: MESCALERO MASK (156110—$2.95)

☐ THE TRAILSMAN #83: DEAD MAN'S FOREST (156765—$2.95)

☐ THE TRAILSMAN #84: UTAH SLAUGHTER (157192—$2.95)

☐ THE TRAILSMAN #85: CALL OF THE WHITE WOLF (157613—$2.95)

☐ THE TRAILSMAN #86: TEXAS HELL COUNTRY (158121—$2.95)

☐ THE TRAILSMAN #87: BROTHEL BULLETS (158423—$2.95)

☐ THE TRAILSMAN #88: MEXICAN MASSACRE (159225—$2.95)

☐ THE TRAILSMAN #89: TARGET CONESTOGA (159713—$2.95)

☐ THE TRAILSMAN #90: MESABI HUNTDOWN (160118—$2.95)

☐ THE TRAILSMAN #91: CAVE OF DEATH (160711—$2.95)

Prices slightly higher in Canada

Buy them at your local bookstore or use this convenient coupon for ordering.

NEW AMERICAN LIBRARY
P.O. Box 999, Bergenfield, New Jersey 07621
Please send me the books I have checked above. I am enclosing $_____
(please add $1.00 to this order to cover postage and handling). Send check or
money order—no cash or C.O.D.'s. Prices and numbers are subject to change
without notice.

Name_____

Address_____

City _____ State _____ Zip Code _____
Allow 4-6 weeks for delivery.
This offer is subject to withdrawal without notice.

Ø SIGNET   (0451)

UNTAMED ACTION ON THE WESTERN FRONTIER

☐ **THE TERREL BRAND by E.Z. Woods.** Owen Terrel came back from the Civil War looking for peace. He and his brother carved out a cattle kingdom in West Texas, but then a beautiful woman in danger arrived, thrusting Owen into a war against an army of bloodthirsty outlaws. He would need every bullet he had to cut them down.... (158113—$3.50)

☐ **CONFESSIONS OF JOHNNY RINGO by Geoff Aggeler.** It was a showdown for a legend: Johnny Ringo. Men spoke his name in the same hushed breath as Jesse and Frank James, the Youngers, Billy the Kid. But those other legendary outlaws were gone. Only he was left, and on his trail was the most deadly lawman in the West.   (159888—$4.50)

☐ **FORTUNES WEST #2: CHEYENNE by A.R. Riefe.** A spellbinding series! As the Civil War ended, cattlemen, sheepherders and farmers in Wyoming vied for the land against the fierce Cheyenne and Sioux. Dedicated officer Lincoln Rhilander had to defy his superiors to rout the redskins ... and had to choose between duty and desire in the arms of a beautiful woman. Stunning adventure!   (157516—$4.50)

☐ **THE SAVAGE LAND by Matt Braun.** Courage, passion, violence—in a surging novel of a Texas dynasty. The Olivers. Together they carved out an empire of wealth and power with sweat, blood, bravery and bullets....   (157214—$4.50)

☐ **THE BRANNOCKS by Matt Braun.** They are three brothers and their women—in a passionate, action-filled saga that sweeps over the vastness of the American West and shines with the spirit of the men and women who had the daring and heart to risk all to conquer a wild frontier land.   (143442—$3.50)

☐ **A LAND REMEMBERED by Patrick D. Smith.** Tobias MacIvey started with a gun, a whip, a horse and a dream of taming a wilderness that gave no quarter to the weak. He was the first of an unforgettable family who rose to fortune from the blazing guns of the Civil War, to the glitter and greed of the Florida Gold Coast today.   (158970—$4.95)

Prices slightly higher in Canada

Buy them at your local

bookstore or use coupon

on next page for ordering.

Ⓞ SIGNET BOOKS

BLAZING NEW TRAILS

(0451)

☐ **THE TERREL BRAND by E.Z. Woods.** Owen Terrel came back from the Civil War looking for peace. He and his brother carved out a cattle kingdom in West Texas, but then a beautiful woman in danger arrived, thrusting Owen into a war against an army of bloodthirsty outlaws. He would need every bullet he had to cut them down.... (158113—$3.50)

☐ **THE BLOODY SANDS by E.Z. Woods.** Jess McClaren's dad owed his life to Joe Whitley, and now Whitley was at the end of his rope. Jess's dad was dead, and the father's debt was now the son's. So Jess arrived on a range where he could trust no one that wasn't dead to pay a dead man's debt with flaming guns.... (152921—$2.95)

☐ **GUNFIGHTER JORY by Milton Bass.** Jory draws fast and shoots straight when a crooked lawman stirs up a twister of terror. When Jory took on the job of cleaning up the town of Leesville, he didn't know it was split between a maverick marshal and a bribing banker. Jory was right in the middle—and he only way to lay down the law was to spell it out in bullets ... (150538—$2.75)

☐ **MISTER JORY by Milton Bass.** Jory's guns could spit fire ... but even he had his work cut out for him when he took on a big herd of cattle and a gunman faster on the draw than he could ever hope to be.
(149653—$2.75)

☐ **DREAM WEST by David Nevin.** A fiery young officer and a sixteen-year-old politician's daughter—together they set out to defy every danger of nature and man to lead America across the Rockies to the Pacific ... to carve out a kingdom of gold ... and to create an epic saga of courage and love as great and enthralling as has ever been told. (145380—$4.50)

☐ **ALL THE RIVERS RUN by Nancy Cato.** Here is the spellbinding story of a beautiful and vital woman—the men she loved, the children she bore, the dreams she followed, and the destiny she found in the lush, wild countryside and winding rivers of Victorian Australia. (125355—$3.95)

Prices slightly higher in Canada

 Buy them at your local bookstore or use this convenient coupon for ordering.
NEW AMERICAN LIBRARY
P.O. Box 999, Bergenfield, New Jersey 07621
Please send me the books I have checked above. I am enclosing $_____
(please add $1.00 to this order to cover postage and handling). Send check or money order—no cash or C.O.D.'s. Prices and numbers are subject to change without notice.

Name_____

Address_____

City _____ State _____ Zip Code _____
 Allow 4-6 weeks for delivery.
 This offer is subject to withdrawal without notice.